Mistletoe and Mischief

A Pride and Prejudice Christmas Anthology

by

Jann Rowland

Lelia Eye

Colin Rowland

One Good Sonnet Publishing
Publishers of Fine Romance
and Fantasy Fiction

This is a work of fiction based on the works of Jane Austen. All the characters and events portrayed in this novel are products of Jane Austen's original novel or the authors' imaginations.

MISTLETOE AND MISCHIEF: A PRIDE AND PREJUDICE CHRISTMAS ANTHOLOGY

Published by One Good Sonnet Publishing

ISBN: 198921214X
ISBN-13: 9781989212141

To my family who have, as always, shown
their unconditional love and encouragement.

A SPRIG OF MISTLETOE

Jann Rowland

Hanging a bough of mistletoe was a common practice in Regency times, as was the custom of catching young ladies under it and stealing a kiss. As I considered this tradition, I began to think of the possibilities involved in Mr. Darcy and Elizabeth being together at a party, not to mention Mr. Darcy continually witnessing Elizabeth's kisses with other men . . . .

"**A** Christmas party at Longbourn?"

"Yes, Darcy, a Christmas party at Longbourn. It is scheduled for tonight. That is the established practice, for people to gather together and partake of Christmas cheer."

Darcy glared at his friend while the man's sister watched behind him, an expression of extreme distaste adorning her features. Caroline Bingley's opinion of the neighborhood could not be misunderstood, and Darcy saw no reason to comment on it.

"Georgiana and I have just come from London, Bingley," chided Darcy. "I do not know that we wish to attend a soiree at Longbourn this evening."

"Oh, do let us go, William," said Georgiana. "It will be so much fun to be a part of the Christmas cheer of which Mr. Bingley speaks."

"Do not expect too much of this neighborhood, dearest Georgiana," cooed Miss Bingley. "In fact, I cannot think of a single person with whom you would be comfortable exchanging more than pleasantries."

"I can," said Darcy without thinking on the matter first. "I am certain you will like Miss Elizabeth Bennet very much, and Miss Jane Bennet—Bingley's intended—is a sweet and gentle young lady, indeed."

The reminder of her brother's recent engagement to Miss Bennet was not palatable to Miss Bingley, who scowled. The reminder that Darcy thought well of Longbourn's second daughter was no doubt even less welcome.

"Miss Elizabeth!" squealed Georgiana, clapping her hands with delight. "That is the young lady whose name you mentioned in your letters to me. Yes, let us go, Brother, for I long to make her acquaintance!"

Miss Bingley's scowl deepened at this further evidence of Darcy's lack of disdain for Miss Elizabeth. "Let us not exaggerate, Mr. Darcy," said Miss Bingley. "Do you wish for your lovely sister to emulate the impertinence of Miss Elizabeth?"

"There is nothing wrong with Miss Elizabeth's manners, Miss Bingley," replied Darcy, recalling with a slight smile the bewitching young woman of whom they were speaking.

"I should say not," said Bingley, fixing his sister with a hard look. "Caroline, you must remember we shall soon be connected with the Bennets. As such, you should refrain from making comments at Miss Elizabeth's expense. Besides, though you have never warmed to her, she is an intelligent and interesting sort of girl, and I have no doubt Miss Darcy will soon become fast friends with her."

Her countenance turning green at the thought of the girl whom she wished to impress becoming friends with another whom she detested, Miss Bingley opened her mouth to retort. Unfortunately for her, her reply was interrupted by Hurst, who, as always, appeared to be insensible of the argument, yet proved a keen awareness of what was happening around him.

"Mrs. Bennet sets an excellent table," said Hurst. "Of course, we shall attend."

Darcy had to suppress a chuckle. Hurst could naturally be trusted to consider the matter with his stomach.

"I know not if our new guests shall attend," said Bingley in reference to the Darcys, his gaze warning his sister to refrain from replying. "For our part, however, I have accepted the invitation. Thus, Caroline, Hurst, Louisa, and I will attend." Bingley turned back to Darcy. "What say you, my friend? There will be nothing to do here at Netherfield should you choose to avoid tonight's amusement."

"Then you leave us no choice," said Darcy, to Georgiana's obvious delight. "Georgiana and I will attend with you."

Elizabeth was not expecting much from the introduction to Miss Darcy. Truth be told, she expected nothing other than the barest civility from any members of the Bingley party—except Mr. Bingley himself—for they had shown themselves to be proud and above their company.

"You should not judge Miss Darcy before you meet her, Lizzy," counseled Jane in advance of their guests' arrival that evening.

"Can it be you expect the proud Mr. Darcy's sister to be anything other than equally proud?"

"I expect nothing, Lizzy," said Jane, an unusual hint of sharpness in her tone. "Rather, I prefer to make her acquaintance and form my opinions based on her behavior."

Jane would, of course, expect the best. In this instance, however, Elizabeth could not say her sister was incorrect. Regardless, there was little reason to concern herself with the girl's behavior, for if Miss Darcy *were* proven to be proud, what would it signify to *Elizabeth*?

"There is merit in what you say," said Elizabeth at last. "Still, Miss Bingley's character suggests that anyone of whom she approves must demonstrate themselves worthy of esteem."

"Miss Bingley is not so very bad, Lizzy."

It was all Elizabeth could do not to roll her eyes. "Jane, though you are now engaged to Mr. Bingley, you know his sisters do not favor the match. Why, they followed him to London with the express desire of keeping him there, and you know he was most explicit in informing you of their arguments against you."

"And I cannot blame them for their opinions," insisted Jane. "We are not of high society, Lizzy, and I do not possess a handsome dowry. I understand what Mr. Bingley is giving up in marrying me."

"As do I," replied Elizabeth, "though I should much rather emphasize what he is *gaining*. Still, it is *his* decision to make, not his sisters'. Nor his friend's, for that matter."

"Mr. Bingley said nothing of Mr. Darcy trying to persuade him against me."

This time, Elizabeth did roll her eyes. "Perhaps he did not. But he has made his opinions clear for all to see."

When Jane gave her a quelling look, Elizabeth laughed and patted her sister's arm, saying: "Do not concern yourself, Jane, for I have no intention of being anything other than gracious and welcoming to Mr. Darcy's sister. I hope, very much, that she is as amiable as Mr. Darcy is not, but I shall reserve judgment until I make her acquaintance at the very least."

Longbourn was not a large estate. It was nothing to Pemberley, and even Netherfield was larger and grander than what Georgiana could see before her. William regarded the estate as if it were somehow dangerous to him personally, and Mr. Bingley's sisters acted as though they were being forced to step into a hovel in which they would not condescend to house their dogs. But to Georgiana, it was charming. Furthermore, she thought she had a notion of why William was so wary of the house before them.

It was gratifying to the shy young girl that the residents were so welcoming to her. Not that she was entirely comfortable, for Georgiana had never been at her best among strangers. But though Misses Kitty and Lydia were boisterous, Mr. Bennet satirical and incomprehensible at times, and Mrs. Bennet loud and flighty, the eldest sisters more than made up for these flaws with their kindness.

"Miss Darcy," said Miss Bennet when Georgiana was first introduced to her. "How lovely it is to make your acquaintance, for we have heard so much of you!"

For an instant, Georgiana looked to her brother for assistance. Miss Bennet's words were an echo of what she had endured from so many other young ladies who flattered her to impress her brother. William, however, was not attending, for he had fixed his gaze on a young woman to whom Georgiana had not yet been introduced. Deciding Miss Bennet had not meant anything untoward with her comment, Georgiana endeavored to respond.

"You cannot have heard as much concerning me as I have of you, Miss Bennet," said Georgiana. "I dare say Mr. Bingley has not stopped speaking of you since the moment I came to Hertfordshire!"

The blush appearing on the lady's face confirmed Georgiana's supposition and delighted her in the process. Mr. Bingley was a good man, and he deserved a woman who cared for him as a man—not for his pocketbook.

After a few stammered and shy replies, Miss Bennet's attention turned to Mr. Bingley, and she all but forgot about Georgiana. Soon thereafter, Georgiana was introduced to the second-oldest Bennet sister. In Georgiana's opinion, the introduction could not have been any better.

"Your brother has had much to say of you, Miss Darcy," said Miss Elizabeth. She then directed an arch look at William. "According to him, it seems you are accomplished at everything to which you try your hand, you are sweet and obliging to all, and you are in possession of the most excellent temper of any young lady in the land."

This time, it was Georgiana's turn to blush. "My brother, of course, exaggerates. He is far too kind to me."

"I am not, Georgiana," said William, giving her a smile. "You are everything Miss Elizabeth says and more."

"Well, Mr. Darcy," said Miss Elizabeth, "it seems you are an excellent elder brother. If your sister is willing to paint such a flattering picture of you, it seems I must allow her the greater knowledge of your character."

"Would you disagree with this representation of my character?" challenged William.

"Oh, I could never be so bold," replied Miss Elizabeth. "It is clear that Mr. Bingley esteems you, as does his family. Now, meeting your sister, I am convinced her sweetness is a point in your favor. I hope to know her better the longer she is in the neighborhood."

At that moment, Miss Elizabeth was called away to assist her mother, leaving the Darcy siblings to watch her as she departed.

"And I hope to come to know *you* better," murmured Georgiana. It was clear her brother overheard her, but Georgiana did not reply to his questioning look.

It seemed Jane was nothing less than correct regarding Miss Darcy, rendering Elizabeth grateful she had greeted the girl with the open-minded acceptance her sister had demanded. Though she might never have expected proud Mr. Darcy's sister to be shy, it was no less than the truth. Regardless, Elizabeth already had decided she liked Miss Darcy very well.

"The decorations of the season are lovely, Miss Elizabeth," said Miss Darcy sometime later as she admired the festive nature of the room. "Oh! And you have a kissing bough!"

"Indeed, we do," replied Elizabeth with a grin. "What celebration of Christmastide would be complete without a kissing bough?"

Miss Darcy turned to Elizabeth, wide-eyed. "Has a gentleman caught you under the kissing bough?"

"Of course," replied Elizabeth, favoring her new friend with a grin. "It is nothing more than a little harmless fun, after all."

At that moment, a grinning Lydia, who had been standing under the kissing bough and casting an inviting smile at Lieutenant Denny, was rewarded when the officer stepped forward, plucked a berry, and gave her a kiss. The hoots of laughter rang throughout the room, much to Lydia's satisfaction. Elizabeth only shook her head. She was not certain it was proper to stand under the bough as an invitation; rather, the gentleman was supposed to catch a young woman passing under it unaware.

"Yes, I suppose it is," said Miss Darcy, looking at it with no little alarm. "I am not yet out, Miss Elizabeth. I am not sure I would welcome a kiss when I am only sixteen."

Elizabeth smiled. At least Miss Darcy showed greater sense than Lydia. "Then you need only refuse the kiss, my dear Miss Darcy. It only means you will not marry in the next year, and as I suspect you do not wish to do so anyway, you lose nothing."

"What of you?" inquired Miss Darcy. "Do you wish to marry soon?"

With a laugh, Elizabeth patted her young friend's hand. "I would not be against it, but I must insist on marrying a man whom I deeply love. Should a man catch me under the mistletoe, I shall agree to the kiss—as long as he is not repulsive—for I wish to keep my options open."

The nod with which Miss Darcy replied was distracted, as if she were considering some other matter. Elizabeth's words were put to the test when, only a few moments later, she was caught passing under the bough by a local gentleman. As he was a man whom Elizabeth had known all her life, Elizabeth laughed and allowed him to kiss her, though she knew very well he had no interest in her as a wife.

As kisses were frequent, the number of berries rapidly diminished, and soon there would be none left to provide opportunities to surprise young ladies with a kiss.

It seemed another party noted the dwindling number of berries, though at first Darcy had little notion she was paying any attention. The festive season rendered the general exuberance of the company somewhat less trying on Darcy's nerves, and as a result, he found himself enjoying this gathering more than was his wont. The opportunity to observe Miss Elizabeth Bennet so frequently also did wonders for Darcy's mood.

"Oh, William!" exclaimed his sister as she came near. "Is this party not so much fun? I declare I have never experienced such a setting as this!"

Darcy glanced at her, noting her glowing countenance and wide grin, and he reflected that even though it had not been his preference to spend the evening in such a fashion, the exuberance of these people had been beneficial to his sister. Thus, he could answer in the affirmative.

"There is one thing I wished to ask you," said his sister after he spoke. "I overheard Miss Lydia speaking of Mr. Wickham a short time ago. Is Mr. Wickham in the neighborhood?"

The scowl with which Darcy met her questions might have induced her to silence in the past. On this occasion, however, Georgiana contented herself with watching him and waiting for a response. Discussion of Wickham was one place Darcy did not wish to go, but he knew his sister would not be content with attempts at evasion, so he endeavored to respond.

"Wickham joined the militia regiment not long before Bingley's ball," said Darcy, noting his sister looking about at the assorted officers as if Wickham might be hiding among them. "There is no need to concern yourself, Georgiana, for Fitzwilliam came to Meryton at my behest and spoke with the colonel here concerning Wickham's character. That libertine shall never again distress you."

Standing nearby, Elizabeth could not help but overhear Mr. Darcy's comments about Mr. Wickham, and her first reaction was to be offended by them. The gentleman, it appeared, would not cease his persecution of the officer, regardless of his own culpability in Mr. Wickham's state of poverty.

Then again, it was unusual for Mr. Darcy to call the man a libertine, as he rarely descended to use such a term in the normal course of conversation. Furthermore, his talk of distress spoke to some further situation with respect to Miss Darcy. The memory of Mr. Wickham calling her proud returned to Elizabeth, and a hint of doubt entered her heart because of it.

Before Mr. Darcy could continue speaking, cheering rose in the room again, for Miss Bingley had taken a position under the mistletoe, her coquettish look at the tall gentleman a clear invitation for him to kiss her. Mr. Darcy, however, either ignored the woman or did not notice her—the latter, if Elizabeth saw aright. But another young man had seen her.

"It seems I have caught you, Miss Bingley," said Samuel Lucas, Charlotte's younger brother. He reached up to the bough and plucked a berry, before leaning in, saying: "I believe I shall claim my kiss now."

Miss Bingley shrunk away with revulsion, exclaiming: "A kiss?"

"Unless you wish to refuse," said the gentleman with a smirk, "in which case you cannot expect to marry in the coming year."

The glance Miss Bingley shot at Mr. Darcy informed anyone watching of her thoughts. However, it appeared Mr. Darcy was not about to save her from the ignominy of being kissed by one of the locals, for he only looked on with amusement. In the end, Miss Bingley accepted her fate, though with little grace and an obvious desire to flee thereafter.

When that bit of excitement had played out, Mr. Darcy and his sister resumed their conversation. Though Elizabeth knew eavesdropping was not admirable, she listened, eager to hear more.

"Do not concern yourself about Mr. Wickham ever distressing me again," said Georgiana. "The only way he shall have power over me again is if I allow him, which I shall never do."

"I am happy to hear you say that, Georgiana," replied Darcy, gazing on her with all the affection of his heart. "It shows you have grown and matured and are now equal to the slings and arrows the world may throw at you. Wickham, however, will not bother again, for I have called in his debts. The place where he is going will be difficult, if not impossible, to return from."

Georgiana nodded and turned back to scan the crowd of revelers before turning a sly eye on Darcy. "Miss Bingley was waiting under that kissing bough for you, William."

Taking a sip of his punch, Darcy said: "Then she will wait for a very long time. Just because a woman is passing under the kissing bough does not mean a man is obliged to kiss her."

With a laugh, Georgiana exclaimed: "But think of the disappointment you are causing her, William! I dare say your indifference will crush her."

"My indifference has never crushed her before," replied Darcy. "I doubt it will do so now. And if I *did* kiss her, I have no doubt it would provoke her to purchase her trousseau."

Georgiana laughed even more. "It is nothing less than the truth, I suspect." She paused, and then, with the greatest audacity, she said: "If you were to marry another woman, Miss Bingley would give up her endless scheming."

"Perhaps she would," replied Darcy. "But I can well fend her off."

At that moment, Miss Elizabeth walked by them, and Darcy's eyes followed her as she went, his sister forgotten. A moment later Miss Elizabeth became the latest lady to be caught under the kissing bough by one of the officers.

"Miss Elizabeth is popular with those looking for a kiss. In fact, I dare say she has been kissed at least three or four times already."

"Perhaps she has," replied Darcy, feeling a hint of jealousy well up within his heart.

"Then it would be best for you to take a chance and claim her lips yourself, Brother. The kissing bough's berries are running out, and you would not wish her to fall in love with someone else this evening."

With a smile, Georgiana turned and walked away, joining a group of young ladies that included Miss Kitty Bennet and Miss Maria Lucas. Darcy was surprised, for he had not thought his nascent admiration for Miss Elizabeth had been noticeable. As another young lady was ensnared under the kissing bough, Darcy idly watched Miss Elizabeth, wondering what her lips would feel like under his. There was only one way to find out, but he was not certain whether he could muster the courage to pursue it.

It was not a revelation, for the conversation had been too oblique for that. Yet the words Mr. Darcy had exchanged with his sister had painted an image of Mr. Wickham which was at odds with how he had presented himself to the company. When coupled with the sweetness of Mr. Darcy's sister, which seemed so contrary to Mr. Wickham's words concerning her character, it left Elizabeth confused.

She decided it was best to leave the matter alone in the end, for it was none of her concern. The effect of what she had overheard, however, left her with a warmer feeling for Mr. Darcy than she had possessed before.

For some time afterward, Elizabeth wandered the room, speaking with several others, generally enjoying what was a wonderful party in her favorite season of the year. The revelers played various games, and laughter was a constant companion. Even her youngest sisters were made happy when several of the officers decided there must be dancing and commandeered Mary to play some music for their entertainment.

It was Miss Darcy, however, who once again set Elizabeth's perception of the evening on its head. It happened as they were standing to the side, watching the dancers as they skipped and hopped their way through the dances.

"Excuse me if I speak out of turn, Miss Elizabeth," said Miss Darcy, "but it seems to me that you are not friendly with certain members of our party."

Elizabeth shot a glance at Miss Bingley, who was sitting with her sister and looking about as if some foul smell had wafted under her nose.

"There are certain members of your party who do not invite friendship," replied Elizabeth, staunchly avoiding any glance at Mr. Darcy.

It seemed Miss Darcy caught part of her meaning, for she glanced at Mr. Bingley's sisters before she raised her hand to hide her giggle. "Yes, Miss Bingley and Mrs. Hurst consider themselves very important. But their behavior should offend you too much, for they are much this way wherever they go."

As Elizabeth watched Miss Bingley, she saw the woman's eyes fall on Mr. Darcy, and with a quick word to her sister, Miss Bingley once again rose. Though Elizabeth saw nothing untoward in her actions, Miss Darcy understood her purpose.

"I wish Miss Bingley would give up this doomed pursuit," said she with a sigh.

Curious, Elizabeth watched Miss Bingley as she made her way across the room, stopping a few times as if to speak with others, though Elizabeth thought no more than two words escaped her lips. Then Miss Bingley with an obvious deliberation of manner placed herself under the kissing bough, looking at Mr. Darcy, who stood only a few feet away.

"Oh, no, not again!" exclaimed Miss Darcy with a giggle.

Much like last time, Mr. Darcy did not react to Miss Bingley's attempt at provocation, but Mr. Lucas was quick to step into the breach. Though Elizabeth and Miss Darcy were far enough away that they could not overhear the words that passed between the pair, Elizabeth noted that Miss Bingley seemed waspish and Mr. Lucas insouciant. He claimed his kiss, and Miss Bingley swept back across the room to sit beside her sister in clear discontent.

"It would be amusing if it were not so very pathetic," said Miss Darcy with a shake of her head.

"But she *is* determined," replied Elizabeth. "I have not known Miss Bingley or your brother for long, but it was evident from almost our first meeting that Miss Bingley wishes to be your brother's wife. It was also immediately clear he does not return the sentiment."

"He never has. William endures Miss Bingley because he wishes to keep her brother's friendship." Miss Darcy paused and turned to Elizabeth, who wondered if she intended to say something momentous. "William has never paid attention to *any* young woman. That is why I was so surprised when he mentioned *you* several times in his letters to me."

Elizabeth raised her eyebrows at that admission. "Your brother spoke of me in his letters?"

"More than once," said Miss Darcy. "And given the way he watches you wherever you are in the room, I must own to surprise that you are not already engaged."

Before Elizabeth could muster a response, Miss Darcy departed under the guise of gaining a better vantage of the dancing. Her words, however, stayed with Elizabeth, putting her off balance.

As Darcy watched the antics of those under the kissing bough throughout the course of the evening, his sister's words kept returning to him. And the more he thought about it, the more he wondered why he did not just follow Georgiana's suggestion. Miss Elizabeth was a comely young woman who intrigued him like no other lady he had ever met, and even if most members of her family were not the sort one would desire to have as relations, there was nothing to say against her.

"I see you are still set on standing about, Darcy," said Bingley after Darcy had pondered the issue for some time. "Are you not enjoying yourself?"

"Quite the contrary, Bingley," said Darcy with an absence of mind. "I am glad you persuaded me, for it has been an enjoyable evening."

"You see, Darcy?" said Bingley with an insufferable look of smugness, "I knew you would come to appreciate my neighbors if you allowed yourself to see them for the good people they are. What about dancing? Miss Elizabeth is still without a partner—surely you will not claim the same nonsense as you did before about her being slighted by other men."

Darcy's eyes had hardly left the woman all evening, and he knew very well no one had slighted her. She seemed at ease with almost everyone in the room.

"No, I would never suggest such a thing," replied Darcy. "But you know I do not appreciate dancing."

"Then you should look to the kissing bough," said Bingley, "for I believe there are only a few berries left. It is the perfect chance to steal a kiss with no further obligation."

Bingley smiled and turned away, leaving Darcy to watch Miss Elizabeth once more. As he did so, Darcy decided there was nothing he wished for more than to discover what it would be like to kiss Miss Elizabeth Bennet. All he needed was an opportunity.

As the evening continued, Elizabeth attempted to watch Mr. Darcy in as unobtrusive a manner as possible. It was difficult to do so, however, for she soon discovered that Georgiana was correct—Mr. Darcy watched Elizabeth as often as Georgiana had said.

Whereas before Elizabeth had always assumed he watched her with prejudicial eyes, she could now see that was not so. While there were times when she was not certain how he felt, she soon realized he did not watch her with contempt. No, there was something else at work.

Could he truly be watching her with interest? The notion was not as repugnant as Elizabeth might have expected. No, instead her mind returned to the first time she had seen him and how she had thought him the handsomest man she had ever seen. Then, she had wondered if he were as interesting as he was handsome. Well, Mr. Darcy had never been *uninteresting*, even when she had considered him to be one of the proudest men of her acquaintance.

The question was: did her new friend have the right of it? Though one might accuse Miss Darcy of bias for a beloved brother, further thought forced Elizabeth to confess that the young woman would have a greater understanding of Mr. Darcy's character than Elizabeth could possess. Should Miss Darcy be correct about Mr. Darcy, then what was Elizabeth to do about it?

In the end, she decided to test the supposition.

Georgiana was delighted! After her last words to Miss Elizabeth, she noted her new friend's distraction for the rest of the evening. Now, Miss Elizabeth watched William as assiduously as William watched her. Could Georgiana finally gain a sister? It was possible, though Georgiana knew a kiss would not prompt William to beg for Miss Elizabeth's hand on bended knee. But it was a good start!

"What do you find so amusing, Miss Darcy?" asked Miss Lydia a short time later.

Though she had been a little wary of the youngest Bennet, Georgiana had warmed to her and now wished she possessed Miss Lydia's confidence. There was nothing wrong with the girl except for an excess of exuberance. Georgiana thought she would enjoy having this girl for a sister.

"Do you not see my brother watching your sister?" asked Georgiana, indicating each of them in turn.

Miss Lydia fixed both William and Miss Elizabeth with a critical frown before shrugging. "It is much the same as usual. Mr. Darcy has often watched my sister. There is nothing out of the ordinary."

"For him to watch your sister as much as he does is itself out of the ordinary," replied Georgiana.

"Do you think he admires her?" asked Miss Lydia, turning to her with surprise.

"I would be very surprised if he does not," replied Georgiana.

"But she is not handsome enough to tempt him!"

"What do you mean?" asked Georgiana, puzzled by the other girl's turn of phrase.

"At the first assembly Mr. Darcy and Mr. Bingley attended in Hertfordshire, Mr. Bingley tried to induce your brother to dance with Lizzy, and your brother declared he would not do so, saying he would not give consequence to young ladies slighted by other men."

Though Georgiana thought it seemed to be the grossest of falsehoods, soon it became clear Miss Lydia was serious.

"My brother said that?"

"Within Lizzy's hearing," replied Miss Lydia. "How can you suggest he admires her, considering that?"

Georgiana shook her head. "I have never known William to speak of a woman in such a manner, so it is difficult for me to know what to think of it. But I am curious—to what do you attribute my brother's propensity to watch her?"

"I cannot say," said Miss Lydia with a shrug. "Lizzy says it is to find imperfections about her and laugh at them."

"That is ridiculous!" exclaimed Georgiana. "If my brother does not like a woman, he ignores her. Have you seen how he responds to Miss Bingley?"

Miss Lydia giggled at her suggestion, pulling Georgiana along with her. "Now that you mention it, I can see your point. Then what do you suggest?"

"It is my opinion that William likes your sister, his initial words notwithstanding. I think I have convinced him to do something about it."

Miss Lydia turned to look at Miss Elizabeth and William, eagerness in her delighted grin. "Then perhaps we shall see something amusing, for I would dearly love to laugh."

When Darcy saw Miss Elizabeth walking nearby, he suffered only a moment's hesitation before he acted on his instinct, allowing his prior doubts and his usual manner of considering every decision to rest. Due to their proximity, he intercepted her the moment she walked beneath the kissing bough.

"Miss Elizabeth," said he, stopping her. "I believe it is my right to claim a kiss."

The woman followed his pointed finger to the bit of greenery hung from the ceiling. Darcy reached up and plucked a berry, showing it to her with a smile.

"I believe I have the last berry, Miss Elizabeth."

"Is that somehow significant, Mr. Darcy?" teased the woman. "I know of no legend which suggests the last berry grants anything special to the man who takes it."

"It means I can kiss you," said Darcy. "And to me, that makes all the difference."

So saying, Darcy leaned forward and captured her lips with his, marveling at their softness, which was beyond anything he had ever dreamed. The applause did not even bother him as much as he might have thought it would, too focused was he on the woman before him.

When he separated from her, Darcy noted her closed eyes, taking great satisfaction in her flushed countenance and reddened lips. Then she opened her glorious eyes and peered at him with clear surprise. Even Miss Bingley's shocked gasp and outraged growl could not tear Darcy's gaze away from the wondrous creature before him.

"It seems, Mr. Darcy," said she, proving she was quick to recover, "that I *am* tempting in the right circumstances."

"Entirely tempting," said Darcy before he leaned forward and captured her lips again. Perhaps it was not proper, for the kissing bough only guaranteed one kiss. But Darcy did not care. It was a stupid tradition anyway.

The End

A CHRISTMAS GIFT
Lelia Eye

This story came from a challenge Jann and I had undertaken some years ago. I can already see the differences in my writing from then and now, but I like to think of this as a sort of light and airy tale that is pleasant and warm, if rather basic.

"*Mr.* Darcy, I should think you were perusing an accounting book rather than participating in one of winter's finest amusements. Your countenance is so grim as to be almost fearful."

Darcy gently slid to a stop so he could pause and look behind him at the approaching Elizabeth Bennet. The Bennets were hosting a small ice-skating party on a large frozen pond on the grounds of Longbourn. The weather was cold enough that most of Hertfordshire's populace could be found seeking warmth and comfort indoors, yet Mr. Bennet's daughters were of sturdy constitutions, and they laughed as they skated around the pond despite the biting wind that nipped at their cheeks and noses with the persistence of an energetic young dog.

Darcy took a moment to observe Miss Elizabeth's expression as she stopped beside him. There was a slight crook in the corner of her mouth that indicated she meant her comment to be taken lightly, yet even had he not seen her face, he would have been well aware of the teasing nature of what she had said.

Though Darcy had only known Miss Elizabeth for a few months, he had spent much of that time observing her, inexplicably fascinated with her arch manner and carefree nature. The only reason he was not indulging in that particular pastime at present was that he found his mind to be consumed by less pleasant thoughts. He had been attempting for a few weeks to convince his friend Bingley it was in his best interest to leave Hertfordshire—and more particularly, Jane Bennet—behind, but it had all been to no avail. Still, Darcy had no desire to concede yet. He did not believe the young woman's heart was truly involved when it came to his friend, and he knew Bingley well enough to realize that a marriage without mutual regard could never bring him happiness. As such, Darcy believed departing Hertfordshire was paramount.

Realizing that Miss Elizabeth expected a reply from him, Darcy inclined his head and spoke. "I will readily admit that ice-skating is not my activity of choice."

With a gesture, she indicated that they should skate once more, and he offered an arm to her. Once she had accepted it, they glided forward, taking the circuit around the pond at a pace that matched the others around them. There was something almost soothing about the sound of skates scraping against the ice, yet Darcy found his dark mood calmed more readily by the gentle weight of Miss Elizabeth's hand on his arm. Suddenly, his cheeks felt warm, and he knew it was not from his exertions.

After a few moments, Miss Elizabeth observed: "Despite your distaste for the activity, you seem to be skilled on the ice nonetheless."

"I was raised in the hills of Derbyshire. I have certainly seen my fair share of frozen ponds. My sister is particularly fond of ice-skating."

Still holding his arm, Miss Elizabeth tilted her head and gave him a glance that appeared to be a mild mixture of surprise and puzzlement. "You . . . care for your sister."

Darcy frowned. "Of course."

The young woman's brow crinkled, and she began to pick up speed on the ice, by necessity causing Darcy to move faster. Though he was technically supposed to lead, Darcy did not complain; rather, he felt almost compelled to smile as he was forced to hasten to keep her hand on his arm. And then when the young woman began to laugh, he felt that he was smiling, unable to stop himself from feeding off her ebullient mood.

"My sisters and I used to race across the pond when we were younger," commented she suddenly. The flush of her cheeks rendered her eyes even more beautiful and mesmerizing, and Darcy felt his breath catch in his throat.

Shaking his head slightly to clear it, he asked her: "Why did you stop?"

"Why, Mr. Darcy, I suspect you know very well that the follies of youth must make way for the demands of maturity."

He laughed, the sound uncommon even to his own ears, and he noted the expression of surprise on her face. "I do not believe you would ever let such a trifling thing as age keep you from any pursuits that interest you."

She chuckled in return. "I suspect you are right, Mr. Darcy. Perhaps I should say, rather, that my sisters were the ones who allowed the demands of maturity to overtake them."

"I think the Christmas season is a suitable time to allow oneself to lapse back into childhood, even if only briefly."

Elizabeth Bennet beamed at him. "Why, Mr. Darcy, your words have the ring of something that I might say! I dare say my penchant for playfulness shall have an influence on you yet!"

There were words he left unspoken: "You have already had an influence on my heart, Miss Bennet." He had fought his feelings valiantly, knowing the improprieties of her family and the inequality of their stations, yet as he continued to glide across the ice with the young woman, he found he no longer cared about why they should not be together; rather, all he could think about was why he wanted that smile directed at him.

A shout caught his attention, and he looked up to watch Bingley tumble to the ice, taking Jane Bennet with him. Fortunately, neither one was hurt; instead, the couple was enveloped with laughter at the situation, even as they struggled to regain their footing. Darcy could not help but notice, however, that Miss Bennet's laugh was much more muted than his friend's.

Miss Elizabeth chuckled as they passed the grounded couple, giving her sister a smile, and then she said to Darcy: "I believe that you and Jane are quite similar, Mr. Darcy."

He looked at her in surprise. "Why might you think that, Miss Bennet?"

"You are alike in manner. Neither of you wears your heart on your sleeve; instead, you keep your feelings to yourself, as one might hide a good hand at cards from any nearby. While such reticence may not do a person any favors in love, I think on the whole it is something to be valued in those who possess truly fine characters."

Considering Miss Elizabeth's words, Darcy frowned to himself. As he came to a curve in the pond that allowed him to look at Bingley and Miss Bennet, he wondered if perhaps Bingley could be right after all. Darcy had been searching diligently for a sign that the eldest Bennet daughter felt any particular favor for Bingley, yet maybe it had been foolish to assume her regard would be displayed in the same manner as that of his friend, whose emotions were never in any doubt. Miss Elizabeth, to his knowledge, had no indication of Darcy's particular preference for her. Darcy could very well have been in error to try to apply Bingley's own personality to a perception of Jane Bennet.

His mood lightened, Darcy replied to Miss Elizabeth at last: "Perhaps you know me better than I know myself."

A laugh and a yell were all the warning Darcy and Miss Elizabeth had before they were sent careening to the ice.

Confusion flooded Darcy's mind as he struggled to sit up on the slick ice, and it did not take him long to realize the reason for his fall. It appeared that Lydia Bennet and one of those infernal redcoats had crashed into him and Miss Elizabeth. Miss Lydia was presently overcome by giggles, and the redcoat, Denny, could not help but chuckle, even as he attempted to apologize to Miss Elizabeth. Miss Lydia did not even bother, so caught up was she in her mirth.

What the two laughing assailants did not notice was the hint of pain on Miss Elizabeth's face; it did not pass by Darcy, however.

"Miss Bennet," said he quietly, "are you well?"

She winced and allowed him to help her sit up. Reaching out to touch her leg, she owned: "I think my ankle is sprained."

Biting back the angry words he wanted to spew at Miss Lydia and her foolish paramour, Darcy instructed: "Take off your skates, Miss Bennet, and I shall assist you back to the house."

Miss Elizabeth did not even bother arguing, which Darcy believed to be testament to her pain. Instead, she began to unstrap her skates, and Darcy endeavored to do the same. He gestured to a servant waiting beside the pond, and the young man came forward to take Darcy and Miss Elizabeth's skates.

Darcy carefully stood on the ice and reached down to help Miss Elizabeth to her feet. They succeeded in getting her upright, but the expression on her face told him that she would not easily make it to the horse-drawn sleigh that waited nearby to take people to the main house.

"Miss Bennet?" asked he uneasily, his breath coming out in visible puffs in the cold air.

"Yes, Mr. Darcy?"

"Might I—might I carry you to the sleigh? I do not believe you will be able to make it on your leg."

She hesitated a moment before inclining her head. "Though it mortifies me to require such assistance, I am afraid you are quite correct. I would be much obliged if you could aid me."

He gently bent and picked her up. She put her arms around his neck for stability, and there was a brief instant where her cheek was pressed against his chest. Her body radiated warmth, and he could not help but smile down at her.

"Lizzy!" cried a voice.

Darcy turned to see the eldest Miss Bennet skating toward him in a panic, Bingley at her heels.

"Are you all right, Lizzy?" asked Miss Bennet.

"I will be fine," said Miss Elizabeth warmly. "I am afraid Lydia knocked me down, and I hurt my ankle. Fortunately, I think it is only sprained, not broken. As you can see, Mr. Darcy is assisting me so that I may return to the house. You need not be concerned."

Miss Bennet lifted her eyes to Darcy's face, and he knew she was studying him, as if to determine whether he was a suitable assistant for her dearest sister. She suddenly nodded in acceptance, and he felt a lightening of his shoulders, though he was still holding Miss

Elizabeth. Considering he had earlier been observing Jane Bennet with suspicion, it was odd that he should now value her approval.

With a slight nod of his head, he began to walk away from the pond, still holding Miss Elizabeth in his arms. Her warmth was comforting, and he could not help but reflect on how she seemed to fit against him perfectly. It appeared that all his efforts to withstand her charms had been in vain. He wondered how he had been living his life before without such a beacon of light in it. His sister Georgiana was all that was good, yet she was shy, and though he doted on her, it was easy for them to fall into silence whenever they were together. Unfortunately, the occasion of silence was simply one more opportunity for Darcy to brood. With Elizabeth Bennet nearby, however, it was difficult—if not impossible—to withdraw into himself.

They reached the sleigh, and as he assisted Miss Elizabeth into it, he could not help but keenly feel the absence of her slight form against him. How could his spirit have become so intertwined with hers without him knowing? Had she any knowledge of the effect she had on his heart?

"Thank you for your aid, Mr. Darcy," said Elizabeth Bennet once she was settled in the sleigh.

He inclined his head, unable to help the smile that touched his face. "It is always a pleasure to assist a fine young lady."

She lifted an eyebrow, a hand coming up to touch his arm in surprise once the sleigh started to move with startling abruptness. She removed her hand quickly, and he wished he could grasp it to him.

"As often as you avoid dancing with young women at assemblies," said she softly, "I should think aiding young ladies to be the thing furthest from your mind. Still, that smile on your face seems to be genuine, though I am not accustomed to seeing you wear such an unguarded expression."

He gave a slight chuckle, earning himself another raised brow. "I am not a beast, Miss Bennet. I do smile when the occasion is appropriate."

She laughed herself, the noise mingling with the ringing bells on the horses' harness. Darcy's first thought was that it was one of the most beautiful sounds in the world. His second thought was an admonition to himself that he was getting too caught up in the jovial spirits that sometimes infected people during the Christmas season. The third thought that came to him was that, for once, he did not care about avoiding even the slightest appearance of foolishness in order to bulwark his pride, and so he began to laugh with her.

When their mirth had run its course and the house was in sight, Elizabeth turned to look up at Darcy. Her cheeks were pink with the cold, and her eyes appeared as if they were shining with joy. For that expression to be directed at him filled Darcy's heart with inexplicable warmth.

"I am glad I sprained my ankle, Mr. Darcy."

"Why is that, Miss Bennet?" queried he with a frown.

"Though I love the opportunity to glide across the pond like a rather large swan rather than fall upon it like a clumsy duck," said she, smiling at him, "I am glad that I had the opportunity to see a different side of you. I fear that silly prejudices had turned me against you, yet I do not think you are so horrid as I had believed."

Though uncertain whether her words should fill him with gladness or sorrow, Darcy smiled back and shook his head. "I do not believe such a thing as a sprained ankle to be a very merry Christmas gift."

Elizabeth's smile only seemed to grow larger. "Mr. Darcy, you must know that a scheme of which every part promises delight can never be successful, and general disappointment is only warded off by the defense of some little peculiar vexation. Had everything turned out perfectly today upon the pond, I should have constantly been comparing today to the winters I have experienced in the past. I think I have instead gained something much more valuable."

"And what would that be, Miss Bennet?"

She grabbed his arm, lightly clutching it. "A friend. That is, of course, if I do not presume too much."

"I would be honored to be known as your friend, Miss Bennet. And . . . dare I say . . . you would never be the sort to presume too much."

Miss Elizabeth looked at him, and gleaning the humor in his eyes, she laughed. "A joke from Mr. Darcy! Shall the wonders of this day never cease?"

He stared at her and thought to himself that the day had been perfect indeed, sprained ankle and all. Though he had initially fought his burgeoning feelings, he now realized that all the money in England could not make him feel as warm inside as one smile from Miss Bennet. And if she had decided she could call him her friend, then perhaps there was hope that he might one day claim the privilege of courting her with her approval and then, God willing, make her his wife.

It had started snowing at the beginning of their sleigh ride, and Miss Bennet tilted her head back, letting the snowflakes fall onto her face. As Darcy watched her, his heart swelling with some indefinable emotion, she told him, her eyes closed: "Happy Christmas, Mr. Darcy."

He whispered back: "Happy Christmas, Miss Bennet."

The End

CHARITY NEVER FAILETH

Colin Rowland

The impression I have of Mrs. Bennet is that of a woman to whom personal status is almost as important as the goal of seeing her daughters married. In this story, I decided to explore what might happen if Elizabeth and Jane were to have separate weddings and how far Mrs. Bennet might go to ensure that both celebrations were truly amazing.

℮lizabeth Bennet tended to behave as a creature of habit, and today was no different. She had risen early, always one of the first in the manor to greet each new day. After dressing, she had made her way down the staircase to the cloakroom for her coat and walking boots. Her plan, on this morning as on most others, was to depart the house and spend an hour or more exploring the many paths and lanes winding around the Longbourn estate. Elizabeth considered time spent out of doors the most rewarding part of her day and counted herself unfortunate on those occasions when she could not partake of this most pleasant of pastimes.

This day, however, did not conform to her established pattern. Upon exiting the cloakroom, her outerwear fastened, Elizabeth looked to the end of the hall and Mr. Bennet's library. The door stood open, which in itself was a strange occurrence at this time of day. To add further to the mystery, light from the room's lamps could be seen flickering, casting dancing shadows against the surface of the hall opposite, while the sound of quiet imprecations and papers being shuffled could be heard nearby, lending a distinct unease to what had begun as a quiet and normal morning.

Elizabeth paused in contemplation. Should she venture to the open door or refuse to assuage the curiosity tempting her forward? To be sure, mystery beckoned, as if with an outstretched arm waving for her to approach. Elizabeth, try as she might, could not recall a past occasion where this door had been intentionally left ajar.

The library was Mr. Bennet's sanctuary, the one room in the manor he could call his own. Whenever he wished to escape what he considered the nonsense which often characterized evenings in the sitting room, Mr. Bennet would retreat to his library. Invitations to the room were rare for the most part, although Elizabeth, as his favorite child, had been admitted frequently.

Yielding to her curiosity, Elizabeth approached the entrance and looked in, unsure of what she might discover. Her father's desk remained where it usually was, but its surface was littered with ledgers, both open and shut. Behind it, his demeanor utterly unlike what she expected to see in his private haven, slumped her father. His head rested between his hands as he shook it from side to side, and Elizabeth could hear him murmuring: "She will bring about the ruin of my family's good name."

Elizabeth remained at the door for a moment, observing her father's distress, unsure whether to announce her presence or to retreat and leave him with his dilemma. The decision was taken from her when, without warning, Mr. Bennet looked up and saw her.

Accepting escape to be impossible, Elizabeth called upon her cheeriest smile to lift his spirits.

"I should have supposed you to be still abed," said she while approaching the desk. "It is most unusual to find you awake so early."

At this, her father looked in surprise to the great clock which stood in the room.

"A new day is upon us already?" asked he. "I became so engrossed in my study of the estate accounts that I lost track of time."

"Is this not a task to be undertaken at month's end?" asked Elizabeth. "More than a week remains until Christmas is upon us, and I know you well enough to understand attending to matters of the estate is not your favorite activity."

"No, I do not relish my financial duties with regard to Longbourn," said Mr. Bennet with a sigh. "I have spent the night studying the records of earnings realized and disbursements made through the year. It is usually a simple task of not more than one or two hours, and with weddings to arrange, I thought I might review the accounts and begin to set aside such funds as are available for the expenses that will surely arise."

"But Papa, morning is upon us, and the sun will soon arise," said Elizabeth. "Is there something amiss? Has the year's harvest been poor?"

"The year has been kind," said he. "The harvest was a boon to the tenants, and the Longbourn accounts have swelled accordingly."

"Then should you not be in a celebratory frame of mind?" asked Elizabeth. "I should think this year above all is one of joy, with Lydia wedded and residing in Newcastle, and Jane and I soon to wed as well. With a household reduced by three, your accounts at next year-end will be fatter, and you and Mama will be happier and blessed with the peace of a more serene household."

Elizabeth's words made Mr. Bennet smile. "It is true that Lydia's marriage brought with it a serenity Mrs. Bennet and I have not enjoyed in many years. No longer am I beset with complaints engendered by her behavior or the gossip of the Meryton busybodies. Furthermore, without Lydia's influence, I shall own that Kitty is becoming a quiet and studious girl. She now accepts my counsel. I believe when she is ready to come out, she will bear the poise and grace her younger sister always lacked."

"Why, then, are you troubled?" asked Elizabeth. "Are you not fortunate in every way? Jane and Mr. Bingley are engaged, though we had once thought it hopeless, and I found happiness with Mr. Darcy when we reconciled in Derbyshire. I would surmise you also find joy in how it has all come to pass. If this is so, whatever can the problem be?"

Mr. Bennet did not at first reply and even avoided looking at Elizabeth. Finally, however, he revealed what had been troubling him. "My concerns arise from the very situation bringing so much joy to Mrs. Bennet. She is beside herself at present, as she has become caught up in preparations for the weddings of her two eldest daughters."

"I have noticed," said Elizabeth. "She speaks only of her increase in stature with three daughters married, and one to the nephew of Lady Catherine de Bourgh, no less!"

"Therein lies the problem," said Mr. Bennet. "Her plans are excessive. Mrs. Bennet considers herself to have been cheated by the fact that she was unable to be in attendance at Lydia's wedding to Wickham. She has been complaining that a loss of face has attached itself to her because of the elopement that foolish girl attempted."

"But Papa," protested Elizabeth, "Lydia did not elope after all; Mr. Darcy prevented it."

"And I owe him a debt I can never repay," said Mr. Bennet. "Your mother, however, has decided only the most extravagant of weddings for you and for Jane, from the ceremonies to the wedding breakfasts themselves, will restore her status among the Hertfordshire elite."

"Neither Jane nor I have made such a request of her," said Elizabeth. "The simplest of affairs will suffice for me, and I am sure it is the same for Jane as well."

"If I cannot constrain her in her preparations," said Mr. Bennet, "there will be no weddings, as I will be consigned to debtor's prison. I am already being forced to cancel the usual feast I provide for our servants and tenants on St. Stephen's Day."

"But Papa," said Elizabeth, "the festivities of this day are one of the most anticipated Christmas traditions at Longbourn. You cannot deny your obligation to the very people who provide the income we depend upon. St. Stephen's Day is more than a simple feast, magnificent though it may be. It is also regarded by all who attend as your acknowledgement of and gratitude for the work in which each engages for the success of the estate."

"It causes me pain to contemplate, but the plans she is making threaten to consume the funds I have at my disposal. I already have merchants inquiring after the extent of the feast we will serve for the wedding breakfasts and asking whether there are any in Meryton who will not be in attendance. The sums being proposed for your wedding alone surpass the income I receive in an entire year, and Mrs. Bennet intends to serve the same foods, if not even more extravagant ones, in celebration of Jane's wedding.

"If she cannot be restrained, there will be nothing remaining for the support of those who remain after the marriages have been solemnized. You and Jane will be in comfortable circumstances, but we shall not. There is also the matter of Lydia and her wastrel husband in Newcastle. She has already written me twice for funds to help them pay their debts. I have given them nothing myself, but Mrs. Bennet has been more than generous in providing them funds from the household account. All the while, she complains to me about my stinginess in providing for my family, never realizing that she is the reason for my so-called miserliness."

Mr. Bennet rose from the desk abruptly and took Elizabeth's hands in his. "Forgive your father his complaints, Lizzy. I know the financial issues of Longbourn are nothing with which you need to bother yourself at such a time as this. Please put my ramblings from your mind and return your thoughts to whatever interests a woman newly in love."

Mr. Bennet then ushered Elizabeth from the room. With a quick kiss on her cheek, he accompanied her to the manor exit and opened the door for her, advising for her to enjoy her morning walk.

After sharing a heartfelt embrace with her father, Elizabeth passed through the doorway and set out on one of her familiar paths. Unfortunately, the quandary Mr. Bennet had presented to her consumed her thoughts rather than the pleasant experience of being outside.

Elizabeth was unsurprised her father had chosen to share his concerns with her. After all, she had always been quite close with Mr. Bennet. Mrs. Bennet, however, was one with whom Elizabeth had never seen eye-to-eye. Furthermore, the profligate spending mentioned by Mr. Bennet had begun to cause Elizabeth anxiety as she considered the ramifications mentioned by her father. She well knew of her mother's tendency to deplete the household budget without thought for cost. It was not unusual for Mrs. Bennet to find herself with a dearth of funds before the month had even ended.

Elizabeth shared a responsibility for the state of affairs in which her father found himself. It was, after all, her wedding, more than Jane's, which served as the impetus for Mrs. Bennet's overindulgence. Elizabeth felt certain Mr. Darcy's lineage as the grandson of an earl was causing the wedding plans to exceed Mr. Bennet's budget. In Mrs. Bennet's opinion, a loss of status would ensue should the wedding of Elizabeth and Mr. Darcy fall short of consideration as the finest ceremony ever held in all of Hertfordshire.

If Elizabeth, as the second daughter, were to receive an extravagant wedding celebration, then Jane, as the eldest, would be the recipient of a much grander observance which would sow jealousy as far away as London. In this, Mrs. Bennet was adamant, and no amount of persuasion from her husband or daughters would change her opinion.

As Elizabeth walked, she pondered the problem, trying to discover a remedy sufficient to preserve her father's accounts while satisfying her mother's need to experience widespread admiration and envy.

The solution began as the seed from a thought questioning the need for such extravagances. From there, it gained in size as Elizabeth reviewed it in her mind. As potential objections were solved, the idea grew and firmed; by the time she returned to Longbourn, she had arrived at the answer she hoped would satisfy both of her parents. Now, she merely needed obtain a promise of support from Jane.

With steps lightened from relief, she threw open the door and bounded up the staircase. Rushing into Jane's bedroom, she swept aside the curtains, allowing morning light to flood the room.

"The day has begun, dear sister," said Elizabeth to Jane, who had pulled the covers over her head.

"It is not yet time to rise," protested Jane as Elizabeth grasped the bedding and pulled it from her sister's grip. "Leave me to enjoy another hour of rest, I beg of you."

"I cannot while the problems facing our family wait for solutions," said Elizabeth. "Dress yourself; I will wait for you at the breakfast table." Turning from the bed, she left the room, leaving Jane to mumble her mild complaints as she did Elizabeth's bidding.

Jane joined her sister in the dining room some thirty minutes later when Elizabeth had just finished her meal. Her countenance did not bear the cheerful expression she habitually wore, but instead one of perturbation, no doubt the result of being roused from her bed at a time earlier than was her usual practice.

"Welcome," said Elizabeth as Jane sat and fixed her with a woeful stare. "As you can see, I have already eaten. I waited for you as long as I could before finally succumbing to my hunger."

"I was tempted to return to my dreams," said Jane, "but curiosity pulled me from the comfort of my bed. Though you mentioned we were facing problems of some sort, I hope whatever you referenced shall be proven to be only minor irritants."

Before Elizabeth could respond, Jane's attention turned to the plate Mrs. Hill had placed in front of her. As she began to eat, her eyes fastened upon Elizabeth, and she waited for an answer.

"The problems we face revolve around our two weddings," began Elizabeth. A noise from outside of the dining room interrupted her before she could finish, and soon Kitty and Mary entered the room, followed by Mrs. Bennet.

"We will continue our discussion once you have eaten, Jane," said Elizabeth, rising from the table. "I will wait in my bedroom."

When Jane entered her room, Elizabeth sat at the writing desk, composing a letter. As Jane waited, Elizabeth completed the missive. She then folded it and placed it inside an envelope bearing the name of "Mr. Fitzwilliam Darcy" on its face.

"You alluded to issues with our approaching weddings," said Jane when Elizabeth turned to her. "I confess ignorance, as I was not aware of any problems."

"I discovered something was amiss only after speaking with Papa," said Elizabeth. "I came upon him in his library this morning as I prepared for my morning walk. Papa stated he was engaged in studying the estate accounts and had been doing so throughout the night."

"It is not unheard of for him to spend additional effort reviewing the twelvemonth past," said Jane. "It is the end of the year, with the new one almost upon us. I have observed his agitation myself as he studies Longbourn's accounts. He voices his opinion of our wasteful behavior and states as fact the surety that he will be sent to debtor's prison."

"I agree he is prone to exaggeration," said Elizabeth, "but our discussion this morning was unplanned. I found him seated at his desk, ledgers open before him as he voiced quiet oaths to himself regarding his current state of affairs. He was unaware of my presence until I made myself known."

"Was there a cause for his troubles? I would presume such a negative attitude happens each year-end. Papa never cares for the state of the Longbourn accounts and always wishes to spend fewer funds in the coming year. We are witness to this display each Christmastide, Lizzy. Why should we attach importance to Papa's complaints this year?"

"This year is not the same as the previous ones," said Elizabeth to a look of confusion from Jane. "We are both engaged to marry in the coming year, and Mama has taken it upon herself to ensure the events are counted as the finest ever held in Hertfordshire.

"According to Papa, she has made commitments to many of the merchants in Meryton concerning decorations to adorn both the church and Longbourn for the wedding breakfasts, not to mention her commitments with regard to the many delicacies she has planned for our guests. I have seen her speaking with Mrs. Hill, and when I inquired as to the reason, Mrs. Hill stated the discussion pertained to the two meals Papa mentioned. There is also the matter of the St. Stephen's Day feast, which Papa has decided he cannot observe this year. He has stated that Mama's commitments have emptied Longbourn's accounts and left him unable to afford the meal."

"This cannot be true," said Jane, distress clear in her trembling voice. "This tradition has been followed for many years. Our tenants and servants alike greatly anticipate this display of honor and affection from Papa. If he were to decide against it, there would be great disappointment. It would cause animosity and hard feelings on the part of many."

"It was while awaiting your appearance that I spoke with Mrs. Hill," said Elizabeth. "My purpose was to inquire as to the veracity of Papa's claims. In the course of our conversation, I was informed that the plans Mama has made are more excessive than Papa is aware. Mrs. Hill told me the cook will be required to prepare food enough to feed all of Hertfordshire, as Mama has extended invitations to everyone in this vicinity. She even plans to decorate the church itself! Mrs. Hill is not yet aware that the St. Stephen's Day feast is to be canceled this year; I can only imagine what the consequences might be should this decision not be amended."

"What is to be done?" asked Jane. "If Mama continues, then Papa—and the Bennet name itself—will become a laughingstock, held in derision by all."

"In truth," said Elizabeth, "these events will be known far and wide and discussed even in London, although for different reasons than Mama envisions."

"What of Papa?" asked Jane. "Is he not able to dissuade Mama from acting upon these misguided notions? If her ideas come to pass, then you and I will be unable to show ourselves anywhere near Longbourn ever again. We must speak with her and convince her of the foolishness of her plans."

Elizabeth shook her head and raised a finger to her lips to silence her sister. "You are as acquainted with Mama's nature as I am. Do you expect we will find success in urging simpler displays to mark the occasions of our weddings? I for one do not think it possible to convince Mama of the error in her designs."

Jane gave a sigh. "I offer my hope, but I am unconvinced of the advisability in attempting to reason with her. What then can we do? We cannot allow Mama to proceed with these ridiculous ideas, and we must restore the Christmas meal to those who depend upon it. If we must cancel the wedding breakfasts, then so be it. I would much rather see Papa's tenants and servants treated with respect than have those funds wasted on a celebratory breakfast we shall forget in a few short years."

Elizabeth knew Jane was suffering pain at the thought of the wedding Mrs. Bennet was planning. In Elizabeth's heart also lay the fear of the reactions from Mr. Darcy and Mr. Bingley upon learning of the public spectacle her mother sought to force upon them. Unlike Jane, however, Elizabeth was not a girl prone to inaction at unforeseen news. She had pondered the dilemma throughout her morning walk and, after her conversation with Mrs. Hill, had arrived at a solution she hoped would be satisfactory to everyone.

Her heart almost broke at the sight of Jane, who appeared to be on the brink of tears over her assumption that the tenants and servants, people whom she held in high regard for their hard work and service to the Bennet family, would be denied the meal they expected and certainly deserved.

"Fear not, my dear sister," said she to Jane. "I have given the problem much thought and have arrived at a solution I hope will be acceptable. It needs only your agreement to implement."

Jane regarded Elizabeth with hope, her countenance lightening at the prospect of rescue from their present situation.

After gathering her thoughts, Elizabeth leaned forward and beckoned Jane to do likewise.

"This must remain between us," said she in a voice quiet as a whisper. "Should Mama discover our plans, she will oppose them."

"I promise to breathe not a word of this to anyone, absent your permission," said Jane.

"My plan is this," said Elizabeth as she began to explain her suggestions to her sister. To Jane's credit, she offered no interruption until the proposal had been laid out in its entirety.

"If you are sure your idea is feasible, then I will support you," said Jane when Elizabeth had presented her plan and responded to Jane's questions. Jane had made suggestions, some of which Elizabeth accepted as beneficial, but the central idea remained unchanged.

"Again, I urge you to discuss this with no one," said Elizabeth. "I have written to Mr. Darcy to request his and Mr. Bingley's attendance at Longbourn on the morrow; when they arrive, we will involve them in our subterfuge." Elizabeth held aloft the envelope she had addressed to Mr. Darcy.

"I will do as you ask," promised Jane.

"Then, I will have this dispatched to Netherfield at once," said Elizabeth as they exited the room. Jane appeared relieved, as her step was lighter, and her countenance had regained its usual cheerful smile.

"Mr. Bingley and Mr. Darcy are here to see you," said Mrs. Hill to Jane and Elizabeth, who sat at the dining room table the next morning consuming their breakfast meal. "I have shown them to the sitting-room."

Upon entering the sitting-room to meet with their guests, Elizabeth said: "Jane and I thank you for your prompt reply to the note we sent."

Mr. Bingley stood from where he had been sitting, while Mr. Darcy, who had been pacing from one side of the room to the other, paused and looked at them.

"The tone of your letter caused us to wonder," said Mr. Darcy. He had a look of consternation on his face that was clear in the firm set of his mouth and the down-turned brows overtop of his eyes. "Mr. Bingley was determined to visit at once upon its receipt; only your request that we call upon you today kept him from having his horse saddled and galloping to Longbourn. What has caused such distress?"

"It is Mama," said Jane before Elizabeth could speak. "As it stands now, Papa is destined for debtor's prison!"

Mr. Darcy's eyes widened in surprise at Jane's statement, while Mr. Bingley gasped.

"Is this so?" inquired Mr. Bingley of Elizabeth, who hurried to shut the sitting-room doors in order to afford them privacy.

"I hope not," said she upon returning, "but he has been fretting over the scope of her plans for our weddings. Mama has her mind set upon hosting a spectacle of enormous proportions, the fame of which will cause jealousy among high society in London. At least, that is what she expects to happen."

"Not an easy thing to accomplish," remarked Mr. Darcy. "Has she voiced the details of her plans to you or Jane?"

"She has not," said Elizabeth. "She has, however, caused Mrs. Hill some concern with the instructions she has imparted regarding the breakfasts to be served on the wedding days. They are to be extravagant and extensive; in fact, she has stated to Mrs. Hill her intention of serving the meal to all of Hertfordshire."

"She is a woman who is proud of the good fortune that has fallen upon her two eldest daughters," said Mr. Darcy in understanding. "She wants to share this bounty with friends and neighbors."

"But she will decorate the church!" cried Jane. "And with no feast for the tenants and servants, all will scorn and deride us."

"Mama has decided the church is to be gaily decorated and filled to the brim with attendees," said Elizabeth in answer to Mr. Darcy's look of confusion. "Furthermore, Papa has decided we cannot host our traditional St. Stephen's Day repast for the residents of Longbourn due to commitments Mama has made to the Meryton merchants with regard to our weddings. Papa fears Mama will have him in prison before the weddings even take place."

Mr. Darcy watched Elizabeth from the chair he had claimed. His countenance, although still troubled, now bore a look of confidence. As he gazed at his fiancée, a slow, knowing smile crept its way across his mouth, and he relaxed, sitting back in the chair with a chuckle.

"What about this do you find amusing, Darcy?" asked Mr. Bingley upon noticing the expression fixed upon the other man's face.

"Indeed," said Jane, looking confused and perhaps even a little hurt. "Christmas is but a week away, and this news will lessen enjoyment of the day for everyone affected."

"During the short time in which I have been acquainted with your sister," said Mr. Darcy, "I have come to appreciate her stoicism when unforeseen troubles arise. While observing her this morning, I have noticed she does not appear panicked at these developments; instead, she is almost serene.

"Elizabeth, please advise as to why this dilemma does not cause you as much distress as it does your sister."

Elizabeth chuckled, her heart warmed by how well this man knew her. "That is because I have decided upon a course of action to ease our problem. Of course, it requires agreement from both you and Mr. Bingley for its success."

"You have aroused my curiosity," said Mr. Darcy when she paused. "Please enlighten us."

Elizabeth studied the others in the room, noting the differences in each as they waited for her to continue. Jane, who sat at the side of the cheerily burning fireplace, wore a look of excitement.

Mr. Bingley, seated beside her, seemed at first to have retained a level of patience, but this began to change as Jane's excitement bubbled over and spread to him. In response to Jane's unintended assault upon his usual reserve, he began to shift and squirm as Elizabeth delayed her words.

Of all those present, Mr. Darcy alone bore a visage suggestive of complete confidence. He sat relaxed in his chair, observing Elizabeth as she prepared to speak. On his handsome face was a tiny smile comprised of the slightest upturn to each corner of his mouth, as if nothing Elizabeth could propose would be a surprise.

"First," said she at last, "Papa must be prevailed upon to keep with tradition in presenting the Christmas feast to Longbourn's residents. We cannot allow him to cancel such an important event."

"While I am in complete agreement," said Mr. Darcy, "I am unsure as to your plan for accomplishing this worthy goal. I have known Mr. Bennet for only a short time and have found him to be immovable once he has reached a decision."

It was now Elizabeth's turn to display a knowing smile. "I will bemoan the planned cancellation of the St. Stephen's Day feast to Mama. I am certain she will raise the issue with Papa, who will rescind his decision just to silence her."

Mr. Bingley, who had sat without adding to the conversation, now interrupted: "But if the funds are not present, then how is Mr. Bennet to present the traditional feast? Would not the expense attached to an event of this magnitude, however justified, hasten Mr. Bennet's financial problems?"

At this, the smile attached to Mr. Darcy's visage grew in breadth until it seemed of a proportion wide enough to touch each ear. "I suspect Elizabeth has not forgotten about this prospect and has concluded her scheming with an appropriate solution," said he with a laugh. "Please continue."

Elizabeth returned the smile with one which seemed in competition to Mr. Darcy's in breadth and enthusiasm. "Jane and I have discussed our weddings and how the preparations for them have consumed Mama to the exclusion of all else. If you and Mr. Bingley are in agreement, we wish to combine the two ceremonies into one. In this way, Papa has only to fund one wedding."

Mr. Darcy nodded in approval. "A sensible idea. It will lessen the burden on your father's means and rein in your mother. Bingley and I have already heard a little concerning Mrs. Bennet's intentions, as they have been noised about by Meryton's merchants. Most find it amusing, but some have expressed mild derision, even referring to her as dotty."

Elizabeth shook her head. "I feared such a thing might occur. This will upset Papa should he discover it. And should we fail to convince Mama of the ridiculousness of her plans, we shall be subject to unfavorable scrutiny by all."

"Mr. Bingley and I have devised a plan to forestall this calamity. We will host the wedding breakfast ourselves, although our vision shall certainly be much more limited than that envisioned by Mrs. Bennet. By doing so, we will relieve Mr. Bennet's anxiety over the cost associated with such an overzealous affair."

"I am afraid Papa will never agree to such a proposal," said Elizabeth. "His pride will not allow him to accept such charity. He already feels indebted for your timely assistance in Lydia's wedding. I thank you for this offer but expect it will come to naught."

Mr. Darcy smiled at Elizabeth's assertion. "We will see," was his only reply as he snatched up her hand and brushed his lips across it before releasing his grip and stepping back.

"Forgive my impulsive display," said he as Elizabeth's cheeks turned a bright red in embarrassment at his astonishing display of affection.

"We must leave you," said Mr. Darcy before Elizabeth could offer absolution for his apology. "Mr. Hurst must return to London and cannot enjoy Christmas with us at Netherfield. Mrs. Hurst is returning with him, and Miss Bingley has decided she would rather celebrate the holiday with them than with her brother."

"That is regrettable," said Jane, although Elizabeth could hear a tone of relief in Jane's voice which betrayed her happiness at the news.

"What of Georgiana?" asked Elizabeth as the two men prepared to leave. "She will not be observing the holiday alone at Pemberley, will she? I had hoped to celebrate Christmas Day with your delightful sister. We have become close these previous few months."

"Do not fear," answered Mr. Darcy, to Elizabeth's relief. "Her carriage will arrive on the morrow."

St. Stephen's Day that year was a time of joy and merriment at Longbourn, surpassed only by the Christmas celebration of the day previous. Mr. Bennet, as the host, was sure to speak with all in attendance. With each tenant and servant, he was solicitous of their health and wellbeing, taking an active interest in their concerns and imparting his wishes for a bountiful year to come.

Elizabeth watched her father, the enjoyment lighting his countenance a welcome difference from the man she had discovered in his library not a week before. Gone were any vestiges of concerns that had weighed him down. Observing him now filled her heart with joy and lifted her spirits in concert with the gaiety which infused the gathering.

"Your father appears to possess no misgivings with regard to the expenditures necessary for the hosting of this feast," said Mr. Darcy. "He looks as if he has not a care of any kind."

A commotion behind her interrupted Elizabeth's reply. Turning, she witnessed Kitty, Mary, and Georgiana involved in a game of Hoodman's Blind with their cousins, whose parents, Mr. and Mrs. Gardiner, sat at a nearby bench watching the merrymaking. With a smile of gratitude for the benevolence toward the youngsters in their care, Elizabeth turned herself back to Mr. Darcy.

"He wears a lighter countenance since your visit to him regarding the weddings. However were you able to obtain his agreement, nay, his blessing, with such ease? I had supposed he would take offence at your charitable proposal, but nary a word of condemnation has he uttered regarding your discussion."

"When Bingley and I called upon Mr. Bennet, we found him to be less than welcoming with regard to our proposal. He was, in fact, adamant in his opposition to our offer to host the wedding breakfast. As father of the brides, he felt it was his responsibility to assume the financial burdens associated with the celebration."

"I know my father is a proud man," said Elizabeth, "What caused him to relent? Try as I might, I cannot arrive at an answer to this question."

Mr. Darcy gave a laugh that echoed through the gathering and captured the notice of more than one of those in attendance. Mindful of the private nature of their conversation, he lowered his voice before responding to her query: "We spoke for the better part of two hours, with neither willing to yield so much as an inch to the other. Not even Mr. Bingley's attempts to soothe Mr. Bennet's wounded pride by proclamation of the fullness of his love afforded us any headway against his refusal to accept what he referred to as unwanted charity."

"You are describing the father I know and love," said Elizabeth. "I might remind you of my warning regarding his stubborn pride."

"Never did I have a reason to forget the caution I was encouraged to take," said Mr. Darcy. "At last, I insinuated the possibility of elopement to solve the impasse. I believe this was the incentive that caused him to reexamine his position. I know he possessed no desire to endure another situation similar to that involving your youngest sister. If something like it were to reoccur, questions would arise in Meryton and elsewhere, and the Bennet name would most certainly be subject to a loss of stature."

Elizabeth regarded her fiancé with an appraising gaze for perhaps a minute

"You are a most conniving man, Mr. Darcy," said she at last with a smile that was soon followed by a laugh. "I will remember this once we are wedded."

"And well you should," said he as he turned to watch the goings-on. Elizabeth could not help but continue to smile as she gazed upon him, secure in the knowledge that they would be perfect companions for each other.

The End

TWELFTH NIGHT STRATAGEM

Jann Rowland

I have written Twelfth Night balls in the past in different adaptations, but I decided to take a new take on this interesting custom. Though the characters are not mentioned by name from the start, the astute reader should quickly identify the characters in this tale and appreciate the thwarting of one detestable woman's efforts.

And then she saw him. A tall man, noble of bearing, lean of form, with piercing dark eyes looking back at her. Had his face not been covered by a mask, it would have been viewed by all as a handsome face, the likes of which would make young ladies swoon and adolescent girls giggle in appreciation. He was looking directly at her. Had the gentleman been able to see through her golden mask, he would have seen flushed cheeks, the effects of a heightened heartbeat upon her countenance.

The rumble of conversation in the room did nothing to remove her attention from the man standing not far from her. It was a Twelfth Night ball, the first the woman in the golden mask had ever attended in London, the city that never seemed to sleep. Visiting her aunt and uncle's house soon after the beginning of Christmastide, she had not thought to attend such a prestigious event as this. But when the invitation arrived for Lord so-and-so's ball to be held on Twelfth Night, she, along with her aunt and uncle as well as her dearest sister, had agreed to attend with unfeigned eagerness. Her sister was now mingling about somewhere in the press, as were her aunt and uncle, but the woman in the golden mask had been standing alone for a short time. The sight of this man caused all other thoughts to flee.

It was inevitable, the way he approached her, as if it had been destined before either had entered the room. As a diminutive woman, she was forced to gaze upward to observe the black-and-red mask the man wore. The feathers protruding from the edges were waving in seeming time with the dancers on the floor, mesmerizing her, as if the sheer presence of his person was not enough. The intensity in the man's gaze caused her breath to catch in her throat, and when he opened his mouth, his voice was deep yet resonant, and it seemed to echo within her very soul.

"May I beg you for the next dance, madam?"

"I should be honored," said the woman in the golden mask. Pausing, she considered the man before her. "Have we met previously?"

The mask did nothing to hide his grin. "Oh, yes, indeed—there is little doubt we have met before."

When the music for the dance began, she found herself escorted to the floor to stand among all the other dancers. Though distracted, she saw her aunt and uncle watching her with a knowing air. Some distance away to the side, her sister had also been solicited for the sets, and while she frowned at her sister and knew something must be done, there would be time for that later.

Never had two souls been so in tune, for the gentleman moved about her as if he were gliding over a sheet of the purest ice, drawing her along in his wake without effort. Every time their hands touched, the woman in the golden mask could feel a spark of energy run up her arm, straight to her heart, causing it to beat a little faster. And when he looked at her, she felt herself melting, her heart beating faster in response to this mysterious man. Oh, should they spend many nights in this exquisite bliss, she would find herself well pleased, indeed!

At length, the sets ended, and the gentleman escorted her to the side of the floor. He gazed about for a moment before turning back to her.

"I do not see your party nearby."

"My aunt and uncle stepped away some minute ago," replied she. "It is likely they saw some acquaintance and left to speak with them."

The gentleman nodded. "Then I shall leave you, for I have a task to accomplish."

The woman in the golden mask fixed him with a smirk. "As have I. But I should like to meet you here shortly, for I have a great desire to dance with you again."

"There is nothing for which I wish more," said the gentleman.

Then he bowed to her and stepped away. She watched him as he departed. There could be no better man in the kingdom, she thought. Yes, she knew she would see him again soon.

"I know you."

The low, menacing voice pulled the woman in the golden mask from contemplation of her partner. When she turned to regard the speaker, she noted a tall woman, bony and spindly, standing nearby and watching her, contempt oozing from her narrowed eyes and affronted stance. This woman's dark hair was pinned on the back of her head, not a hair out of place, tied with such firmness it must have been pulling her face tight with it. Covering her face was one of the most garish masks to be found in London, a discordant concoction of greens, blues, purples, and blacks that had been topped with a pair of long feathers standing up like sentinels. As if that were not enough, the woman wore a headdress of even greater feathers, giving her the appearance of a particularly thin ostrich—though her personality more closely resembled a vicious raptor.

Though those attending the masked ball were not to know the identities of one another, the woman in the golden mask would have known this raptor anywhere, for there was no other like her. It was well she could not be duplicated, for no one else known to the woman in the golden mask mixed such great measures of pride, conceit, arrogance, disdain for others, and eagerness to climb society's ladder in one person.

"I knew it must be you," said the bird-like woman when no response was offered. "It astonishes me to find you have the audacity to show your countenance at an event of this nature. How did you manage to sneak in undetected?"

"In fact," said the woman in the golden mask, "no one can see my face, so I am hardly ;showing my countenance,' as you suggest. Furthermore, my aunt and uncle are well known to his lordship and have been counted among his dearest friends for many years. The more apt question is: how did you manage to gain an invitation yourself, considering your position in society?

"Oh, you were able to come only due to your connections to a certain gentleman, of course," said the woman in the golden mask before a reply could be given. "It is always under his auspices that you are included in events of this nature, for you do not have the standing to gain entrance on your own merits."

"How dare you!" snarled the other woman, her feathers waving in the air as testament to her rage.

"How dare you?" asked the woman in the golden mask, more amused than offended.

"I will have you know I have been a member of society in good standing for many years now. If I were to ask the host about your presence, would he corroborate your story? Perhaps I should speak to him."

"If you even *know* him, I welcome you to try," rejoined the woman in the golden mask. "Then again, since I doubt you have ever been introduced, no avenue exists for you to speak with him unless you mean to breach all pretense of good manners."

"As your cousin did at my ball?"

"I am not my cousin," replied the woman in the golden mask. "As I *have* been introduced to his lordship, all you will accomplish by approaching him is to make yourself appear the fool. Then again, it would not be an appearance but rather the reality. Is that not so?"

Offense rolled off the raptor of a woman in waves, and for a moment, it seemed as though she might make a scene. Then she calmed herself with a visible effort, no doubt wishing to refrain from drawing attention to herself.

"Perhaps I will speak to his lordship later. I do, however, have one question for you before I see to your eviction."

"Do ask. This has been a rather entertaining conversation."

The bird-like woman's eyes narrowed in anger again. "Impertinent and insolent to the last. Tell me—is your sister here, along with your *tradesman* aunt and uncle?"

"Why, do you wish to apologize to her for your behavior? Are you remorseful for the way you have abused her trusting nature and have feigned friendship when you intended none?"

"Answer me at once!"

"It is none of your concern," said the woman in the golden mask. "I will not allow you to injure her sensibilities again. You had best leave."

"Your designs are not hidden from me," hissed the harpy as she stepped close. "I have anticipated your sister's wish to entrap my brother. I shall not allow your family to win!"

"Then you will do as you must. As will I. Now, leave me be, or we shall see *who* his lordship will support in a dispute between us."

With a stiff neck and a sniff of disdain, the woman moved away with a haughtiness not unlike the ostrich she resembled, leaving the woman in the golden mask grateful to be free of her, though the cloying scent of her perfume lingered in the air. Putting the recent incident from her mind, the woman in the golden mask began to look about the room, trying to spy her sister. She was already late in locating her.

Her sister, it seemed, was not enjoying the evening. It was no surprise, however, as the young woman had been in dull spirits since the autumn, pining away for her lost love. She had agreed to come to London with great reluctance, but it was fortunate that she had, for she would recover more quickly in the bosom of her aunt and uncle's house, where she would receive a respite from her mother's ever-present lamentations concerning the departure of her daughter's beloved.

"Come, Sister," said the woman in the golden mask. "Let us move this way, for I wish to speak to you."

Without comment, the other young lady agreed, allowing the woman in the golden mask to lead her to a more private location. When they arrived, the woman in the golden mask turned to look at her sister, noting her seeming disinterest. Pursing her lips, she decided against commenting upon it, determining instead to be cheerful.

"How are you enjoying the evening thus far?"

"As much as any other dance we have attended," said her sister, the tone of her voice decidedly muted.

"It is a wonderful evening, is it not?" asked the woman in the golden mask. "We have never seen its like in Hertfordshire!"

"No," came her sister's quiet reply, "we have not."

"Take heart," replied she, fixing her sister with a wide smile. "There might be a young man who interests you here tonight. Why, I might even say it is possible you will meet a certain special someone here."

Glancing around, the woman in the golden mask found the tall gentleman from earlier approaching from the other side of the room. He had another man with him this time, a gentleman with reddish hair and what would have been a lively step if he had not been so cast-down in his demeanor. A grin fell over her face as she waited with anticipation for the two gentlemen to reach them. Then, to her annoyance, her sister, oblivious to what was about to occur, started to move away.

"I wish to speak with our aunt," said she by way of explanation over her shoulder.

"Jane!" cried the woman in the golden mask. "Please wait with me here for a few moments. We shall speak with our aunt later."

But Jane did not listen, choosing to ignore her call. Grinding her teeth together in aggravation, the woman in the golden mask stopped and listened to the conversation between the two men nearby, and she realized the taller man had seen what had happened and was improvising.

"It would be a much more pleasant evening if you would dance," said the taller man.

"It would be much more pleasant if I were in Hertfordshire," said the man with reddish hair. He sighed and added: "Then again, I suppose it would not be."

"I urged you to go to Hertfordshire, if you recall."

"You did. But Caroline assures me I would not be welcome."

"When have you started to listen to your sister?"

"All you have is a belief to support your view. Caroline informs me Miss Bennet told her without disguise of her lack of interest in me. Would you have me believe she is lying to me?"

That is exactly *what you should believe!* thought the woman in the golden mask, indignation welling up in her breast. But she knew the man's companion would not make so open an accusation, and she waited to hear how he would respond.

"This setting is not the best for such conversation," said the taller man. "Instead, I believe you should dance and remove your mind from your troubles. Should you wish it, I shall see you again tomorrow and inform you of my opinions in more detail."

"This is rich," said the newcomer with a laugh. "*You* are attempting to induce *me* to dance? Who ever heard of such a thing?"

"Who, indeed?" asked the tall man. "Well, what do you say? If you look in that direction," said he, gesturing at the woman in the golden mask, "there is a lovely young lady who does not have a partner at present. I myself have danced with her and found her quite agreeable — and more than handsome enough to tempt me."

The woman in the golden mask had to cover the giggle that escaped with her hand, but it seemed the man with reddish hair did not understand the reference. He glanced at her with interest, but no spark of recognition could be seen in his eyes. Then he turned back to his friend.

"I dare say she seems very agreeable. At present, however, I should not like to dance."

"Come, my friend. It shall be for the best."

"I have not even been introduced to her!"

"That is the silliest thing I have ever heard you say!" exclaimed the taller man. "Why, this is a masquerade ball, and everyone is hiding behind masks. On this one night, propriety might be relaxed and a woman's hand solicited without an introduction. I insist!"

"Oh, very well," said the second man, though with little grace.

Steeling himself, as if he were about to perform some unpleasant duty, he squared his shoulders and approached the woman in the golden mask. "Madam, might I request your hand for the next dance?"

"Of course, sir," said she, shooting an amused glance at his companion.

Her partner for the next dance looked at her, and what she could see of his brow through the eyeholes in his mask furrowed, as if he were attempting to remember something. In the end, he said nothing, and as the next dance was about to start, he offered his hand and guided her to their places in line. The music started, and they began the intricate steps.

The woman in the golden mask glanced at the tall man standing to the side as she moved, noting him watching her, his eyes seeming to tell her to practice patience. Though she felt quite amused by the circumstances, she knew Jane's happiness depended on the outcome of their charade, so she decided it would be best to follow the directive given to her. For about half the dance, she did not speak with her partner, though she could feel his eyes on her, as if she were a particularly perplexing puzzle.

"Excuse me, madam," said he at length. "Have we met before?"

Laughing at his confusion, she said: "Do you think we have, sir?"

"It is on my mind that we have," replied he. "There is something . . . I cannot even understand it myself. But something informs me you are familiar to me."

"Perhaps we have met, sir. To be honest, I wonder if I should be insulted that you did not know me at once."

"Know you at once?" asked he, his voice rising. "How could I with these damnable masks confusing us?"

"How, indeed? It seems we must use something to aid us other than the pure recognition of putting a name to a face. There are other clues, are there not? Those clues are even now informing you that you recognize me without viewing my features."

"Are you always this teasing?" asked the man, his voice filled with curiosity and only a hint of asperity.

"Nearly always," said she. She was enjoying herself immensely. "My sister has often told me I am far too teasing, and I must own she is, as always, correct, for I dearly love to laugh."

Those words, which had been used more than once in this man's presence, provoked him to start in surprise. While the recognition of her words was evident, however, it seemed he still could not quite place them.

"Look at my eyes, hear my voice, and pay heed to the way I move about this dance floor, sir. Perhaps more importantly, while I believe you recognize *me*, I am also convinced you recognize in me an echo of one you once loved—one whom I hope you still love, for it will lead to great happiness for more than yourself if you do."

With an utter start where he faltered for an instant in the steps, his eyes widened until the whites filled the eyeholes of his mask. Then he righted himself and looked on her with wonder.

"Miss Elizabeth Bennet?"

"You know I should not confirm or deny your suspicion, sir."

The man grinned at her teasing and acknowledged her hit. Then he looked about the room with new seeming passion and interest, his eyes searching. Then he turned back to her and fixed her with an eager and pleading look.

"Is . . . Might I ask if this other of whom you are an *echo* is present tonight?"

"That is a safe assumption," replied Elizabeth with glee. "Had she not determined to find my aunt when you were approaching us a few moments ago, you might have greeted her."

A shadow fell over his eyes. "Did she not wish to see me?"

"There are few she wishes to see more," said Elizabeth. "She did not realize you were present."

A nod, distracted and short, was his response. As they danced, Elizabeth found herself facing the area where the tall man stood watching them, and she noted his scrutiny. When she winked at him, she knew he had understood, if indeed he had not already seen the change in posture of his friend himself. Then Elizabeth saw her sister entering the room from where she had exited and coming near the tall man, only to pause and glance around with a slight listlessness in her demeanor.

Though Elizabeth turned to her companion to point her sister out to him, it seemed he had noticed Jane the instant she had entered the room, as if he possessed a compass which pointed directly toward her. This was a man in love. A man who would be firm to his purpose.

Elizabeth had worried for his resolve, fearing that he would believe the words of his detested sister. That worry vanished in the blink of an eye. What she saw before her very eyes was a testament to his determination—she knew nothing would ever separate them again.

When the music faded away a moment later, the arm her companion offered to her was almost perfunctory in nature. In directing her toward the side of the floor where her sister now stood, he demonstrated an eagerness to join Jane there, to once again make her acquaintance, to love her properly as he had wished to do before. But they were not allowed to proceed without opposition, for a tall, thin figure decked out in feathers interposed herself in their path and attempted distraction.

"Brother," said the bird-like woman after raking her eyes over Elizabeth's form in contempt, "I wish to go home. Let us retire from this place at once."

"If you wish to return home," said the gentleman, "then you may find Louisa and ask her to see you home, for I have no intention of leaving."

The eyes behind the mask flared, and she glared at her brother. "I wish to return home, Charles. You will escort me from this place."

The laugh with which the gentleman responded was harsh and filled with contempt. "Why must we leave at this moment, Caroline? Do you fear I shall discover your lies?" His sister did not respond at once, allowing him to continue. "Did you ever speak with Miss Bennet about me? She never told you of indifference to me, did she? It was all nothing more than a lie meant to separate me from the woman I love, was it not?"

"You would do well not to listen to whatever *this* woman has told you, Charles," spat Caroline Bingley.

"She has told me nothing," said her brother. "But my eyes have been opened to your selfishness and your disdain for the feelings of anyone else, including me, your own brother. You will not control me any longer. I am my own master and will act as I please."

The woman glared at him with contempt. "So, you will ruin my prospects of marriage with your foolishness? *That* is true selfishness."

"Be gone!" growled Mr. Bingley, stepping close to his sister. "I have half a mind to turn you out and allow you to fend for yourself with your own dowry. Whatever the case, I shall no longer listen to you."

Then he sidestepped her and led Elizabeth to the side of the room. For an instant, Elizabeth thought Miss Bingley would move to intercept them again. It seemed, however, that some well of discretion led her to the understanding that she would not control her brother any longer. Elizabeth shot her a triumphant grin as she passed, but while Miss Bingley saw it and was infuriated by it, she was rendered impotent and unable to respond. A moment later, Miss Bingley stalked off in high dudgeon.

The reunion between the two divided lovers was all Elizabeth had ever desired. Jane, overcome with emotion, wept for joy, while Mr. Bingley informed her, as sensibly as can be expected of a man violently in love, of his lifelong devotion and his intention to never again be separated from her. Though a ball might have been an inappropriate place to propose, Elizabeth thought for a moment he would. Instead, he settled on asking Jane for the next, soon leading her away, leaving Elizabeth alone with the tall man at her side.

"Well, that appeared to work quite well," said he, an undertone of mirth in his voice. "I almost had to drag him here, for he was as intent on staying away as his sister was just a moment ago."

"You made a wonderful job of it, sir," said Elizabeth. As she watched Jane and saw her renewed spirits, a sense of contentment welled up in Elizabeth's heart. "Perhaps we might have avoided months of suspense if you had simply kidnapped him and returned him to Hertfordshire. One look at her was all it took."

"Bullying him to stay here where he could come across her was difficult enough. I would not like to hold him in a carriage with a pistol pointed at him all the way to Hertfordshire."

Elizabeth laughed and turned to him, noting the amusement dancing in his eyes. "I now understand what you said of his sister, for I thought she would try to impale me with her eyes when I first spoke with her. Just now, however, I thought she was ready to commit violence."

"That was nothing to compare with how she behaved when she discovered I had been in Hertfordshire most of these past months. Returning there and leasing Pulvis Lodge was the best decision I ever made, for it allowed me to obtain my heart's desire."

"And mine," said Elizabeth. "I suppose we should feel sorry for Miss Bingley, for this has resulted in her dreams being dashed to pieces before her very eyes."

"Her dreams never had a chance of coming true," replied he, looking at her with his heart in his eyes. "My soul cried out for you — only you. I could never have been happy with *her*."

"I am glad to hear it."

"Now, since this is a dance, I believe we should adhere to the forms, my dear. Let us dance again."

Elizabeth gaped at him, feigning shock. "But we have already danced once! It is not done to dance again so soon, sir. So lacking are you in the knowledge of proper behavior, I think I should call you Mr. Collins."

One elegant eyebrow rose behind his mask. "Do you compare me with your foolish cousin?"

"I suppose I should not," said Elizabeth with a grin. "You know the steps better than he."

"Then let me remind you of where we are — this is a costume ball. It is perfectly acceptable for us to dance the night away together."

With a smile, Elizabeth reached for his proffered arm. "In that case, I should be delighted to accommodate your wishes, Mr. Darcy. Let us do just that."

The End

MR. COLLINS'S SPIRITED ENCOUNTER

Lelia Eye

I must confess to having a lot of fun with this one. My mother always loved the Christmas Carol story, and I have seen many different iterations of it. I debated between putting Lady Catherine or Mr. Collins in the role of Scrooge and ultimately decided the latter would likely be more humorous.

*M*r. Collins had no interest in spirits. The only spirit with which he had any involvement was the Holy Spirit, and that was only insofar as making reference to the Holy Spirit in his sermons. However, even his references were filched from other sources, a necessary evil given how many of his instructors and fellow parsons droned on about the need for one to be filled with the Holy Spirit. His understanding beyond that point was rather limited, but he had not yet seen cause to further enlighten himself since the aforementioned lack had never had any detrimental effect upon his life.

It was because of this lack of belief in the existence of spirits that what occurred later seemed so miraculous. However, before those events can be canvassed, it is necessary to learn what preceded them.

Upon hearing of his Cousin Bennet's grave illness a few days before Christmas, Mr. Collins had deemed it prudent to immediately extend an olive branch to the Bennet family, with whom his deceased father had been estranged, and stay with them for a fortnight during the Christmas season. After all, if Longbourn — his cousin's estate — were soon to come to Mr. Collins's hands, it would be helpful for him to have a passing familiarity with it.

Mr. Bennet's impending death certainly could not have come at a more fortuitous time, for Mr. Collins's patroness, Lady Catherine de Bourgh, had passed away a few months before. While the living that had been bestowed upon him belonged to him for life, he felt a distinct sense of loneliness at the parsonage, for he no longer received invitations to dinner at Rosings Park and had no companions with whom to engage himself. Various issues concerning the inheritance of her ladyship's estate were still being resolved, and it was yet to be seen whether the estate's new owner would appreciate the benefit that Mr. Collins's presence brought to the area. If Mr. Collins could only gain an estate to call his own, it would serve as an excellent distraction from his woes and allow him to put her ladyship's demise behind him.

"Yes, cousin," thought Mr. Collins as he considered the person of Mr. Bennet in his mind, "it would be best if you could be so kind as to pass from this world promptly so that I may comfortably establish myself at Longbourn."

The notion of inheriting an estate also brought with it the realization that the estate would need a mistress, and as his cousin's daughters were unmarried and rumored to be quite handsome, it seemed natural for him to plan to select a wife from among them. Then he would have done his familial duty by them and could rest peacefully at Longbourn, knowing that Mr. Bennet's daughters and wife would live with the humble knowledge of their savior's sacrifice toward them.

Shortly after he arrived at Longbourn and made his acquaintance with the Bennet family, he found himself drawn aside by Mrs. Bennet. The woman seemed pale and bordering on hysterical, but as they conversed and she realized they were both in agreement that he should wed one of the Bennet daughters, an aura of calm descended over her. Moments later, she revealed that she had a strong opinion as to which of her girls should become his bride.

"Mr. Collins," said she, "I must warn you most fervently that you must not propose marriage to Jane. There is a Mr. Bingley at Netherfield who is expected to offer for her at any time, and she would be forced to turn you down. That certainly would not do. No, no, the one you *must* ask to marry you is my second-born, Elizabeth. *She* shall make a fine wife for you. Indeed, she has assisted my husband with Longbourn's finances on occasion, and she is knowledgeable of any issues with the tenants. There can be no doubt that she would be a valuable asset for any master of Longbourn should Mr. Bennet leave us soon."

Mr. Collins had considered protesting at first. After all, should he not marry the eldest and most handsome of his cousin's daughters? However, he was soon forced to own that a few minutes' acquaintance *had* convinced him that Elizabeth Bennet was handsome in her own right, and if she did indeed possess the understanding promised by Mrs. Bennet, she should be the most suitable wife once Longbourn fell under his control. Even Lady Catherine would have approved of the woman, though unfortunately he could never manage to confirm such due to her ladyship's most unfortunate demise.

Once he had decided his course of action, he determined it was necessary to reassure Mr. Bennet of the modest yet enviable future that awaited his second-oldest daughter.

"Mr. Bennet," said Mr. Collins by the man's sickbed, "I want to advise you that you may pass comfortably from this world as soon as may be, knowing that the fate of your daughters is secure. Indeed, I have come to impart this most blessed of knowledge upon you, for I can readily say that Miss Elizabeth finds herself in the most enviable position of having been selected as the recipient of my affection and most delicate attentions."

Mr. Bennet gave a small cough and then squinted up at his bedside visitor. "You must forgive me, but I am afraid I do not catch your meaning, Collins."

"Of course, of course. I beg your pardon for not having been clearer. In short, for I understand that long conversation can be difficult to follow for one who is so very ill, I have decided that Miss Elizabeth is to be my future companion in life."

Mr. Bennet was quiet for a few moments as he considered what had been said. "You wish to marry Lizzy?"

"That is correct, Cousin. She shall be comfortably situated in her childhood home for the rest of her days. I am told your eldest daughter is unavailable, but I believe Miss Elizabeth will be a suitable alternative, and I am most pleased to have selected her."

"Have you . . . asked Lizzy to marry you?"

"I have not," said Mr. Collins, "but I am certain that an announcement shall be made ere long. After all, a proposal is but a paltry detail in matters of such import as this."

Mr. Bennet did not appear to be exulted by Mr. Collins's news, but as he soon descended into a fit of coughing, Mr. Collins deemed it prudent to leave the room and allow the man to rejoice in private.

While Mr. Collins might have allowed some time to become better acquainted with a young woman before proposing marriage to her had the circumstances been different, he did not know how long Mr. Bennet was for this world. Believing it necessary to secure Elizabeth's position as his future wife to ease Longbourn's transition from Mr. Bennet's hands to his, he endeavored to secure her hand without delay.

Mr. Collins, though he still had not refreshed his clothes after his journey, entered the drawing-room where the female Bennets sat. Somber looks were worn by all, and the eyes of Miss Bennet and Miss Elizabeth held the redness of recent tears. Seeing him enter, Miss Elizabeth curtsied and then immediately made as if to leave the room, no doubt to resume her place at her father's sickbed now that Mr. Collins had finished with the gentleman.

"I would like to request a few minutes to speak with Miss Elizabeth," said Mr. Collins hastily and loudly, bringing the young woman's steps to a halt.

"Of course," said Mrs. Bennet. "Come, girls! Let us give Lizzy and Mr. Collins a little time alone."

Her brow furrowed in concern, Jane Bennet began: "Mama—"

Mrs. Bennet interrupted her before she could say anything further. "You need not worry, Jane. Simply return to Mr. Bennet's side; he will appreciate the company."

"I should be much obliged if you would do so," said Mr. Collins, bowing.

Mrs. Bennet then continued to usher all her daughters from the room, though not before Miss Bennet had made one last attempt to protest. Once the young women were all gone, Mrs. Bennet closed the door, shutting Mr. Collins inside the room with the quiet Miss Elizabeth.

Though Mr. Collins would have viewed being left alone with a young woman as a most inappropriate circumstance, he knew that exceptions could be made for a proposal, which would, indeed, be most unorthodox to make in a roomful of watching eyes.

"Miss Elizabeth," said Mr. Collins, "please have a seat."

His cousin looked toward the door briefly before she sat on the edge of the nearest chair. "Might I ask why you wish to speak with me, Mr. Collins? As our acquaintance can be measured in no more than a few words, I should wonder why you might feel the need to converse with me in such an intimate fashion."

"Certainly, certainly, I understand the confusion that has come over you, and I shall enlighten you ere long. But this is something I must not rush. In the future, you shall remember this day and think of it quite fondly, I assure you, so I must tend to every detail as a gardener tends to the flowers under his care, pulling out the weeds and sprinkling generous amounts of water to enable his charges to grow as he desires.

"Now, as you know, your father is quite ill, and it is widely believed that he shall not survive until the new year. Upon his death, the estate of Longbourn shall fall onto me due to the entail that was set in place generations ago. I am certain you must be aware of this."

"Mr. Collins—"

"Miss Elizabeth," continued Mr. Collins, "you must accept my condolences for the difficult situation you are in, losing your father as you shall soon. I know how dear the familiarity of an old face can be. But you need not fear also losing the familiarity of your childhood home, and that is the joyous news I bring you."

Miss Elizabeth, who appeared to have been fighting the urge to weep, dabbed at her eyes with a handkerchief and bit her lip. Then she inhaled deeply and said: "Mr. Collins, as I am quite distraught at present and wish to return to my father's side, I would request that you please speak plainly and briefly."

"Very well. As I said, I bring you most joyous news. I have selected you among your sisters as being the one most worthy of taking the position of my future wife. You may wipe away all your tears now and rest peacefully with the knowledge that you need not fear the vagaries of the world. Instead, you will be so fortunate as to be content with your place at my side for the rest of our days."

"Mr. Collins," said Miss Elizabeth, her voice shaky and filled with some sort of emotion that Mr. Collins could not discern, "I appreciate the kindness of your intentions, but I am not convinced that either of us is capable of making the other happy through marriage."

"Miss Elizabeth, I fear you have no choice but to accept me. While I understand this is a difficult time for you—"

"No!" cried Miss Elizabeth. "You do not understand. You cannot know the love that I have for my father or the place he has held in my life all these years."

"The place of your father shall be filled by your husband—"

"No, I cannot agree! Mr. Collins, please—I cannot think of marriage right now. I cannot."

Then, tears streaming down her face, Miss Elizabeth leaped to her feet, flung open the door, and fled the room.

Mr. Collins, after passing a moment of stunned silence, rushed after Miss Elizabeth, nearly colliding with Mrs. Bennet and her daughters, who had been standing outside the door.

"I beg your pardon," said Mr. Collins, dipping his head, before he continued to follow Elizabeth Bennet.

The young woman left the house, sobbing and seemingly moving forward with no destination through the grass. Mr. Collins, though already puffing a little in his exertions, cried out: "Miss Elizabeth, please return to the house!"

They continued in this manner for a few minutes, with the distance between him and Miss Elizabeth growing all the while. Then the sight of a man approaching on horseback slowed both of their steps.

As the horse and its rider drew closer, Miss Elizabeth came to a halt and turned away, wiping at her eyes with the handkerchief she still had in hand. Mr. Collins, his chest heaving with every breath, took the opportunity to move closer to her.

The new gentleman soon dismounted, his face the very picture of concern. "Miss Bennet, whatever is wrong? Who is this man? Is he harassing you?"

Miss Elizabeth finally turned to look at him, fighting to keep her tears and her voice under control. "This man is my c-cousin, Mr. Collins."

"We are in the midst of a very important conversation, sir," said Mr. Collins, "so we would both be much gratified if you would please allow us some time alone to reach a resolution."

"I believe I am speaking to the young lady," said the gentleman coldly.

He then turned to the young woman and asked: "What has he done to you, Miss Elizabeth?"

"Oh, I do not w-wish to marry him!" cried the young woman before collapsing to the ground and sobbing, her face buried in her hands.

"Her father is dying, sir," said Mr. Collins, "and I have merely presented an option that should be welcomed by all. She has been overcome by various emotions, and there is no need to concern yourself."

"I told you I am speaking to the lady," snapped the other man. "I have not made your acquaintance yet and do not desire it."

Then the man knelt beside Miss Elizabeth and gathered her into his arms, cradling her head against his chest and rubbing her back while murmuring comforting words.

"I apologize for my cousin's behavior," said Mr. Collins with a frown, "but your current actions are not appropriate. As her future husband, I believe that I am to be responsible for her well-being, and I shall convey her back to Longbourn."

To Mr. Collins's agitation, the other man ignored him, and once Miss Elizabeth had reached a calmer state, the man stood up with her in his arms and began striding forward, obviously intent on returning her to Longbourn himself.

Mr. Collins watched him for a moment before grabbing the nearby horse's reins and following him with token protests.

Upon their arrival at Longbourn, Mrs. Bennet waited inside near the entrance. At the sight of the gentleman holding Miss Elizabeth, she made a noise of surprise. "Mr. Darcy! Whatever are you doing here?"

"Mr. Darcy?" echoed Mr. Collins. "Why, could it be that you are the Mr. Darcy who is the nephew of the late Lady Catherine de Bourgh? I apologize, for I did not recognize you. I saw you only from a distance at her funeral, you know—"

"Miss Elizabeth is unwell," said Mr. Darcy to Mrs. Bennet. "I believe she needs to rest."

"Of course," said Mrs. Bennet, looking at the young woman. "Let me call for our manservant."

Once Miss Elizabeth had been deposited safely into her bed, Mr. Darcy left after exchanging only a few brief words with Mrs. Bennet outside her daughter's room. To assuage his curiosity, Mr. Collins approached his hostess and asked her about the circumstances which caused Mr. Darcy to be found nearby.

"Mr. Darcy is a friend of Mr. Bingley, the young gentleman who let the nearby estate of Netherfield before Michaelmas," said Mrs. Bennet. "Mr. Darcy has been at Netherfield for a few months with his friend, and he was recently joined in Hertfordshire by his sister so that they might spend Christmastime together."

"How fortuitous that I should meet him here," said Mr. Collins, smiling. "Once he realizes the connection between us, he shall no doubt be glad to bestow his blessing on my marriage to your daughter."

"I would not be so very certain myself," said Mrs. Bennet, "for the man's pride is quite unseemly."

Before Mr. Collins could respond, the housekeeper, Mrs. Hill, appeared and brought a young woman forward.

"Mistress, I hope you do not mind," said Mrs. Hill to Mrs. Bennet, "but Miss Lucas has come to call on Miss Elizabeth and was most insistent upon seeing her after hearing she felt unwell."

"Of course, of course," said Mrs. Bennet, waving for Mrs. Hill to leave. She then proceeded with making the introductions between Miss Lucas and Mr. Collins, explaining that Miss Lucas was one of Miss Elizabeth's dearest friends.

After the introductions had been completed, Miss Lucas told Mr. Collins: "I have tried to call at Longbourn every day since Mr. Bennet became ill. There may not be much that I am able to do, but I try to manage what I can."

"That is quite admirable," said the man, smiling to himself and looking upon Miss Elizabeth with approval. It seemed only fitting that his bride-to-be would have such a considerate friend. He had done well indeed in selecting his future wife.

The next day was Christmas Eve, and when Mr. Collins went to break his fast, he found Elizabeth Bennet waiting for him.

Her face appeared pale, no doubt due to the emotional upheaval caused by her father's illness, yet she spoke to him in an unwavering and almost flat voice. "I have thought about your proposal, Mr. Collins, and as long as you agree to allow my mother and sisters to stay at Longbourn after my father's death, I shall agree to marry you. Though my mother has hoped Mr. Bingley would ask for Jane's hand, I have not yet seen evidence of his commitment to such a course of action, and I cannot be assured that my family will have a place to stay after my father's death unless you offer one."

Mr. Collins smiled. "Of course, Miss Elizabeth. I shall gladly offer your sisters a place to stay until they are married or able to seek positions as governesses, and your mother shall no doubt assist you when it comes to your assumption of duties as mistress of Longbourn. I have reason to believe that our marriage shall bring happiness to all, and you need not fret about the future in the slightest."

Miss Elizabeth curtsied and then left him. Mr. Collins smiled and congratulated himself on handling everything with such promptness.

That evening, Mr. Collins found himself in the highest of spirits when he left the drawing-room to return to his bedchamber. Now, the only item left for all his plans to come to fruition was for Mr. Bennet to pass from this world.

Smiling to himself, he reached out to grasp the doorknob to his room when the face of Lady Catherine de Bourgh suddenly sprung into his vision, emblazoned on the brass of the knob.

With a cry and a muttered oath, Mr. Collins jumped backward, running his hand over his face in surprise. As he looked once more at the door, he found that the knob bore not even the slightest resemblance to his former patroness. Still, he wiped his brow and bowed. "I beg your pardon, your ladyship. Please forgive this humble clergyman for his ill treatment of your person, but I really must enter my room."

Then, carefully watching to ensure the head of her ladyship would not materialize once more, Mr. Collins reached out and turned the knob, exhaling in relief as it retained its ordinary shape.

"Seeing Mr. Darcy recently must have stirred up memories of her ladyship's funeral," said Mr. Collins to himself, attempting to explain away the unnatural occurrence. "I must have been imagining her on account of our meeting."

Shaken despite his attempt at justification, Mr. Collins proceeded in readying himself for sleep and putting on his nightclothes. But once he had drawn the bed linens back and proceeded to sit upon his bed, a voice called out his name sharply.

"Mr. Collins!"

He jumped and looked up at the frowning visage of his former patroness. "Lady Catherine!" Gasping, he pulled the bed linens up over him like a shield. "What . . . Whatever happened to you?"

He had failed to notice it at first, but her ladyship was completely covered in chains. They crisscrossed all over her body in a tangled mess, and they were so numerous as to make it impossible to tell what she wore underneath. Even her head had a crude sort of hat upon it that had been formed from links of metal. As Mr. Collins continued to stare at her in stupefaction, he realized that she was also transparent and hovering at least a foot off the ground.

"You wish to know what happened to me, Mr. Collins?" asked Lady Catherine with an upturned lip, rattling her chains as if to emphasize her point. "I forged every one of these chains by myself through my officiousness. By trying to force everyone to do as I wished rather than allowing them to live their own lives, I neglected to fill myself with the milk of human kindness and instead filled myself with the poison of selfishness."

"I beg your pardon, your ladyship, but attempting to encourage others to abide by your wishes is not against the Commandments—"

"Selfishness is not to be abided, Mr. Collins, and selfishness ruled my entire life.

"But just as I am covered with these chains, so, too, are you fettered. Your chains may not be so long and great as mine, but they shall grow every day until you reach the afterlife and find yourself to be choked by them."

Alarmed, Mr. Collins looked about him to find the chains her ladyship had referenced, but he saw nothing. Even running a hand about his neck failed to find a solitary link of metal. "I beg your pardon, your ladyship, but I do not see any such chains."

"You may not be able to view them now, but they are there, Mr. Collins."

"But why?" asked Mr. Collins. "Why should I have any chains at all?"

"Is it not true that selfishness and your sense of self-worth rule *your* life, Mr. Collins?" asked Lady Catherine. "When you asked Elizabeth Bennet to marry you, were you trying to do what was best for her or what was best for *you*?"

Still holding up the linens to obscure her ladyship's view of his nightclothes, Mr. Collins stammered: "Our marriage would be mutually beneficial—"

"Collins!" snapped Lady Catherine. "Your proposal was hasty and careless of Miss Elizabeth's feelings. Beware how you act in life, or else you shall forge your own chains in death. I would suggest that you mend your ways with Elizabeth Bennet immediately, or you shall be forced to suffer the consequences."

"Your ladyship," said Mr. Collins, bowing forward until his forehead touched the bed, "I can assure you that the circumstances are quite different from what you seem to believe. As such, you need not worry for my well-being, though I am, of course, touched that you would make a special visit after your death for the mere purpose of assisting your humble clergyman."

"Heed my words, Mr. Collins, before your chains are so tangled together they can never be removed," said Lady Catherine ominously, clanking her chains together before her transparent form dissipated entirely.

Mr. Collins stared after her vanished form for a few moments to ensure she would not immediately reappear. Then he reached forward and grabbed his nightcap, which had fallen off while he was bowing. Shakily, he placed it upon his head, and then he sank backward into his bed. After gazing around the room once more, he closed his eyes, attempting to calm himself and lose himself in dreams.

He awoke abruptly sometime later—it could have been minutes or hours—to find a new pale figure at his bedside. He gasped as he realized the identity of his newest visitor. "Miss de Bourgh!"

The meek figure of Anne de Bourgh gazed down at him, her countenance pale even for a spirit. Mr. Collins had not known her long, for she had passed away a few months before her mother. Some believed the two deaths were connected—that Lady Catherine let go of life out of grief for her daughter's death—but Mr. Collins had not joined anyone in making such speculations.

"Mr. Collins," said Miss de Bourgh quietly in greeting.

"Might I ask why you are here, Miss de Bourgh?" asked Mr. Collins. Truly, he could not understand why he had been called upon by one spirit, much less two—particularly since he had not even believed they existed!

"I have come to show you the dangers of forcing someone to acquiesce to your wishes."

"While I am not quite certain of what precisely you mean, I should not think that it would be a trial for anyone to abide by the desires of an upstanding clergyman such as myself."

"Do you believe that Elizabeth Bennet truly had need of your interference? Do you believe that she wanted to marry you?"

"I believe she made the choice most befitting of her situation. When her father passes from this life, her mother and sisters shall need a place to reside, and I have eased her concerns for the future, as her husband-to-be should. Perhaps she has not had time to develop feelings of affection, but I shall make up for that lack during the remainder of my stay. There shall be no cause to repine."

"What of her sister's anticipated engagement?"

"I know not the circumstances, but as the engagement has not yet occurred, it may not come to pass, so I do not believe it worth considering at the moment."

"Could you not have inquired further?"

"I saw no reason to do so," said Mr. Collins. "After all, marriage to me shall be an incredible gift, even more impressive than the prospect of marriage to another gentleman in the area. Miss Elizabeth shall never have to leave her home, and her mother and sisters will be secure in their futures. What more could she desire from marriage than that?"

"Have you considered why Miss Elizabeth rejected your proposal at first?"

"It is my understanding that such coy ways are the heart-blood of young women during these times. They feign disinterest at first before finally surrendering to what is natural and desirable."

Miss de Bourgh pursed her lips. "I suspect you shall not see where you have erred even if I ask you a thousand questions. Very well. Let me show you something instead."

The spirit stepped toward him, and he forced himself not to flinch. She passed her hand in front of his face, and he closed his eyes at the movement. When he opened them, he found himself immersed in new surroundings.

"This is . . . this is the home where I was raised," said Mr. Collins, looking around in awe. "I must be in the midst of some strange dream."

He moved from the entryway and walked forward, taking in the modest surroundings which he knew so well. His father had been a miser, embittered by a hundred grievances but also desirous for his son to reach a comfortable station in life that would give him the right to sneer at Mr. Bennet, with whom he had become determined to remain on poor terms. As the elder Mr. Collins disliked the expense of private tutors, that meant his son was often under his strict guidance; as he was illiterate, that meant the situation was almost always nigh unbearable for both him and his son. He could scarcely teach, and his son could scarcely learn from him.

Thus it was that Mr. Collins found his steps stilled entirely when he came upon a familiar scene.

A portly young boy sat at a small desk, quill in hand as he flinched in response to the lecture being hammered down upon him by a stern man whose face had the look of one who never smiled.

"William!" spat the man. "You know how important this letter is, yet all you have succeeded in doing is covering the page in ink blots and something that scarcely seems as if it can pass as writing. We cannot afford the expense of page after page of paper. Utilize the sides and write as small as you possibly can. I shall not let your blunders cost us anything further."

There was a pause in which the boy murmured a plethora of apologies as he worked, and then the man said: "Foolish boy! Have you no brains in that thick skull of yours?"

"I apologize, Father," said the boy, bowing his head and apologizing over and over again.

As Mr. Collins looked upon this young version of himself, he felt a heavy pressure in his chest. As his father could not read and write, letters had always fallen to the younger Collins. Still, in spite of the elder Collins's lack of understanding, the man would always supervise his son's correspondence, critiquing anything he possibly could and forcing his son to read the letters time and time again to ensure they said exactly what was intended.

His breath caught in his throat as he wondered whether he could be seen and heard by the two figures from his past.

"This scene is one your father repeated many times," said Miss de Bourgh, moving to stand at his side. "You need not be concerned, for they do not know you are nearby at present. What has happened here is immutable."

"Ah, yes, of course," murmured Mr. Collins.

"As a boy, you were berated constantly. You would apologize over and over. Your father chose everything for you, from your shoes to your career.

"We are not dissimilar in this way. My mother also dictated my life for me. Just as I confined myself to my home out of my mother's desire to aid my health, so did you become a clergyman at your father's insistence. Neither of us dared to dream our own dreams."

Mr. Collins looked at the vision before him, at the unhappy boy simpering and apologizing, the angry man growling and criticizing. Miss de Bourgh's words disturbed him on some level, but he could not quite describe the reason.

He took in a deep breath and pushed his shoulders back as he tried to shake off the emotions conjured up by this glimpse into his past. "Perhaps it was not my choice, but my impeccable character was formed through my father's efforts."

"Impeccable, you say?" returned Miss de Bourgh. As he looked at her, ready to question her disparagement of his character, her form disappeared before his eyes.

He gawked for a moment, running his hand in front of his face, only to jump in surprise as his father, who he had believed to be standing before him, appeared beside him.

"Ah, w-what?" stammered the younger Collins, scarcely knowing what to say. "You—I thought you were—were you able to see me before now?"

"William," said his father gruffly, "I can see you at present, and only that signifies."

"Might I inquire as to why you are here still, sir?"

"I have something to show you."

"Might I inquire as to what that might be?"

The elder Collins did not answer verbally. Rather, he gestured for his son to follow, and he strode forward and walked through the bedchamber door without opening it.

Mr. Collins gaped after his father for a moment before he tentatively took a few steps. He put out a hand to grasp the doorknob, but his fingers passed through it. He swallowed, took a deep breath, and walked through the door, shivering as he did so.

The elder Collins had not slowed to allow for any delay, so his son had to hurry to reach him.

"Am I a spirit as well?" asked the younger Collins in a slight panic. "Have I passed away in my sleep?"

"You are not dead," said his father, "but it would be better for Elizabeth Bennet if you were."

"I do not understand—"

As his father walked through the door to Mr. Bennet's bedchamber, Mr. Collins had no choice but to follow him.

The room bore two figures, but not the ones whom the younger Collins would have expected. Mrs. Bennet must have been sleeping elsewhere, as Mr. Bennet was the only one in the bed. Beside him, her head bowed over his hand, was Elizabeth Bennet.

However, she was not asleep. Instead, she sobbed quietly, her shoulders shaking with the effort to subdue any noise.

"Ah, my dear Elizabeth," said the younger Collins, moved by the sight before him. "She must be deeply affected by the knowledge that her father shall soon depart from this world, just as a good daughter should be."

"That is not the only reason for her tears," said the elder Collins. "Because of her sense of responsibility, she has agreed to marry a man whom she can never love."

It took a few moments for the meaning of his father's words to enter Mr. Collins's head. "I beg your pardon?"

"William," said his father, "you are not the sort of man who could ever make Elizabeth Bennet happy. She should be with a man who can challenge her intellectually and elicit full and deep feelings of affection."

"I fail to see how you have come to this sort of expectation—"

"Have you actually had an in-depth conversation with the young woman? Are you aware that her preference in books is vastly different from your own? Have you come to realize that she takes heart in the exertion of long walks in the countryside?"

"No, I suppose I—"

"You have scarcely taken the time to speak to her, much less look at her. I may not have done right by you as a child, William, but I can at least say without prevarication that I loved my wife. I would have given the world to her, and the insult that your cousin Bennet gave her—"

The man cut off and shook his head. Once he had gathered his wits about him again, he said: "Well, once she died, I felt I could never forgive him, and you suffered for it as well. That was one of my greatest mistakes. But the son need not willingly make others suffer for the sins of the father."

The younger Collins, watching Miss Elizabeth sob, felt his heart deeply touched by the sight of her plight. Still, he told himself: "I can soothe her tears. She shall be much better situated upon assuming the position of my wife, and she shall find herself with no cause to regret her new life."

As he continued to gaze at her, he thought her to be quite handsome despite her tears, and he wondered why he should not be granted the honor of looking upon her face every day.

Eventually, he realized the ghostly figure of his father had disappeared. After looking about him to ensure that the man had not simply stepped to the side, Mr. Collins left the room with the intention of returning to his bedchamber. When he stepped out, however, he nearly cried out in surprise. There, standing in front of him, was his cousin Bennet.

"Mr. B-B-Bennet," stammered Mr. Collins, looking back at the door to the room where he had just seen the man. "Are you—have you passed—that is, *are you no longer with us?*" This last was said in a mere whisper as Mr. Collins looked furtively around.

"I regret to inform you that I have not yet departed from this world," said Mr. Bennet. "I know you must be quite despondent to hear it."

Mr. Collins bowed a few times. "I should never venture to speak of despondency at such a time as this, Mr. Bennet."

"Of course."

"However, I do wish to inquire as to the reason for your appearance at this time. Should you not be abed?"

"What I should do and what I actually do are ofttimes contrary to one another," said Mr. Bennet, "but that does not signify. I appear before you with a singular purpose tonight."

"I suppose there is something that you wish to show me," said Mr. Collins, recalling the previous ghosts who had called upon him.

"Indeed," said Mr. Bennet. "You have already seen glimpses of the past and present, but I am here to show you the future."

Mr. Collins smiled broadly in anticipation. "Ah, certainly, certainly, that would be a most logical assumption, would it not? I confess that the future is the period of my life that I am most desirous of witnessing. I wish to see that most felicitous bliss that must lay before me."

"I suppose you might not have any anxieties about the future at present, no matter what you may have seen this night, but I do wonder whether you shall be so cavalier once you finally return to your bedchamber."

"Have you a scene for me to witness?"

"I do indeed. However, I think mine might have the greatest effect of all. Certainly, I hope it shall."

"I should be honored to see whatever a dying man might wish to show me," said Mr. Collins. He soon realized his words might not be taken in the light he meant them, and he bowed and said, "Ah, beg pardon, sir."

"No offense taken, Collins," said Mr. Bennet, waving his hand. "In fact, I rather find that the subject of death seems a fitting one."

The older man waved his hand once more, and Mr. Collins's surroundings faded out of view and then suddenly came sharply in focus. Mr. Collins glanced around and realized immediately they were outside. "This is . . . ?"

"Longbourn Cemetery," said Mr. Bennet, "a place where the dead are quite comfortable in their rest. However, I believe the person whom you would find to be of most interest is over there."

Mr. Collins looked at the place where Mr. Bennet gestured, and he saw Miss Elizabeth seated in front of a headstone. Her body shook, and Mr. Collins shook his head sadly. "Ah, she must be crying due to your demise, Mr. Bennet. She is quite the filial young woman—"

"Actually, Mr. Collins, I would suggest you look again."

Mr. Collins moved forward to gain a better vantage, and he quickly realized Mr. Bennet was quite correct in indicating that the situation was not as it first appeared. Rather than crying, Miss Elizabeth was laughing as she played with a young girl, teasing her sides and eliciting ecstatic giggles.

Mr. Collins frowned. "This is unusual behavior in a place where the dead are interred."

"It is," said Mr. Bennet. "However, the passing of a particular person has brought her great joy."

"Joy?" echoed Mr. Collins. "It is rather odd that a young lady should be in such a state after someone has passed from this earth."

"Well, the death of the person in the grave before you has brought her great freedom. She is no longer bound to the whims of another but free to do as she will."

A sickening feeling took residence in Mr. Collins's gut. "What of the young girl? Is that her daughter?"

"Yes, indeed."

"Her daughter does not appear to be afflicted by the passing of . . . this person."

"The little girl takes after her mother. If her mother is not saddened but rather filled with joy, would not the daughter be so as well?"

"They are playing at a *grave*," said Mr. Collins, his tone almost entreating. The sickening feeling only worsened.

"Did you not feel the same sense of overwhelming relief at the passing of your father? Would you not have played at his grave had you been younger when he left this world? After all, you were no longer beholden to his will. He never saw you as his equal, and he would have continued to control your life."

"Whose grave is this, Mr. Bennet?" whispered Mr. Collins. He knew the answer, of course, but he had to hear it.

"Have you not looked at the name upon the marker?" asked Mr. Bennet in a tone that was almost mocking. "Why, it is yours, Mr. Collins."

Mr. Collins looked away, wringing his hands together as he felt himself beset by an unbearable agony. He felt as though he had suddenly been stabbed through the heart. "I do not wish for my wife and child to rejoice at my passing."

"What man would?"

"Is this the future that must come or merely a future that could be?"

"The future you see before you is not set in stone," said Mr. Bennet. "There is still time to undo what has been done. I think perhaps there is another young man who might make my daughter happy."

"Another young man?"

"Mr. Darcy has appeared to show a particular interest in Elizabeth of late. I believe he would make a much better match for her."

"Then I know what I must do," said Mr. Collins in a rush, his decision abruptly made. "Thank you, Mr. Bennet. Thank you for leaving your sickbed to keep me from making a most grievous mistake. I had no notion I was forcing Miss Elizabeth into so unsuitable a position. You may be assured I will correct it at once!"

He bowed a few times, and he felt that sensation of the world blurring around him before he found himself once more in his bedchambers. He remained still for a few moments to orient himself before he realized he was sitting up in his bed. Had he been asleep and only now just awakened?

Mr. Collins reached out and ruffled the blankets on his legs, testing his ability to manipulate his surroundings. The level of light in the room indicated it was morning, so he must have awoken from the dreams that had so moved his heart.

He leaped out of bed, shoving the first pair of shoes he found on his feet and then running from the room. He rushed outside Longbourn and was surprised, but pleased, to find Mr. Darcy approaching on horseback.

"Mr. Darcy!" cried he, rushing forward and waving his arms to catch his attention.

The gentleman continued forward, and once he drew close, he dismounted. "Mr. Collins," said he, speaking more cordially than he had at their last meeting, "I might inquire as to the reason for your unusual appearance. Has something happened to the Bennets?"

"No, sir," said Mr. Collins, waving a hand dismissively. "Rather, I am vastly pleased to see you this morning, for I felt most desirous of speaking with you."

"I also believe I might have some business with you," said Mr. Darcy, his voice and posture suddenly stiff.

"Ordinarily, I should gladly listen to whatever business with which you might flatter me, but the issue which I must discuss with you is one that cannot be further delayed."

"Mr. Collins, I wish to discuss your marriage to Miss Elizabeth—"

"No, no, Mr. Darcy," said Mr. Collins. "There is to be no marriage! I have decided—I cannot be dissuaded—there is nothing that can change my mind—Miss Elizabeth and I do not suit, and I shall not marry her. I must insist that you take her to be your wife."

Mr. Darcy remained silent for several moments, his mouth partway open, as if he had meant to speak but forgot what he had intended to say. Finally, he asked: "I beg your pardon? How did you know that I was coming to—"

"I do not know whatever your business is this morning, sir, but I fear you must leave off it at once and propose to my cousin. I have come to realize that you may be able to make her happy and that I shall not make a good partner for her. I will not have her, Mr. Darcy. I do not want her any longer."

Before Mr. Darcy could respond, the door to the house opened, drawing their attention. The subject of their discussion walked outside, only to pause and pale at the sight of the two gentlemen.

"Mr. Darcy, Mr. Collins," said the young woman, hastening into a curtsy.

"Miss Elizabeth," said Mr. Collins, stepping toward her, "might I inquire as to the state of your father's health this morning?"

She glanced at Mr. Darcy before returning her attention to Mr. Collins. Subdued, she said: "He appears to have a little more strength than he did yesterday, so I intended to take a brief walk around the house before returning to be with him."

"I confess I am somewhat surprised to hear that he still breathes this blessed air," said Mr. Collins, "but I am glad for it, indeed, for you have a most important business to attend to with him this morning."

"Mr. Collins," began Mr. Darcy.

"No, no, you must attend to it immediately. I shall not hear of anything else."

Once someone had been called to see to Mr. Darcy's horse, Mr. Collins ushered his cousin and Mr. Darcy into Mr. Bennet's room.

"Mr. Collins," said Miss Elizabeth, her voice sounding somewhat strained, "I beg your pardon, but I am not aware of what sort of business it is that Mr. Darcy could have with my father at this time."

"My dear cousin," said Mr. Collins, bowing and smiling, "you shall find out soon enough. I have faith that Mr. Darcy shall acquit himself well."

He stepped out of the room and quietly shut the door. After glancing around to ensure no one else stirred at this early hour, he placed his ear against the door. While he ordinarily would not scruple to eavesdrop, he felt this matter concerned him so closely he had little choice but to listen to ascertain whether circumstances proceeded as they should.

"Well, Mr. Darcy," said Mr. Bennet, "I suppose you at least have some notion of what was alluded to by Collins."

"I do," said Mr. Darcy. "I had wished to talk to your daughter in private first, but I suppose there can be no help for it now."

"What is your business, then? Surely you shall not keep a man on his sickbed waiting."

There was a brief pause before Mr. Darcy spoke once more. "The simple truth is that I wish to marry Miss Elizabeth. Before you protest, I must emphasize that my love for her is most ardent and sincere. The thought of her marrying a man who cannot appreciate her mental faculties has sickened me. I am confident that I can bring her the happiness that Mr. Collins cannot."

"I beg your pardon, sir, but my illness appears to have afflicted my hearing. Could you please repeat yourself?"

After Mr. Darcy expressed himself once more, Mr. Bennet exclaimed: "Well!"

"Mr. Darcy," said Miss Elizabeth, "you are aware that I have already agreed to marry my cousin—"

"Mr. Collins releases you from your promise," said Mr. Darcy. "He no longer wishes to marry you, but I certainly do."

"Now, Mr. Darcy," said Mr. Bennet, "while I can say without exaggeration that Mr. Collins is not the sort of man whom I would want to marry my most intelligent daughter, I do know that she would have at least been on an equal footing of sorts with him.

"You may find it surprising to hear, but I am actually aware that you have been harboring feelings toward Lizzy. Despite the rumors that have passed throughout the neighborhood, my illness was not sudden, so as it has come over me, I have attempted to watch those who might be interested in my daughters. I have been a foolish man, not investing as I should, but I do nonetheless desire that my family be cared for after my demise. It is because of my careful attention that I have witnessed the way your eyes follow Lizzy's movements and soften at her laughter. While I am aware that you are capable of providing for her, you must know that there is little in terms of connections and dowry that she shall bring to a marriage. As such, I am not certain she is well-suited to be the wife of such a prestigious figure as yourself."

"I have money and connections aplenty," said Mr. Darcy. "What I desire is a wife whose wit and vivacity shall bring mutual happiness to us both. I can promise you that I shall do everything I can to make your daughter happy. I have always wanted to love my wife as my father loved my mother, but I never actually expected to have the opportunity to find such a gem as she.

"If you agree to give your daughter in marriage to me, I promise that I will do whatever I can to make her love me as much as I love her."

"Handsome words from a young man, to be certain," said Mr. Bennet, "but I must confess I remain hesitant. Are you certain you want *my* Lizzy for your wife? While I believe she is worth more than any other young woman in England, I know your family must have certain aspirations with you in mind."

"I suspect you are more than aware that the worth of spirit and mind should outweigh any other considerations. As such, Mr. Bennet, you must consider giving your blessing. My mother—" Here, Mr. Darcy paused, and he seemed to consider whether to continue saying what he had intended. Finally, he did, though in a soft voice that Mr. Collins had to strain to hear. "My mother visited me in a dream last night, and she told me in no uncertain terms that I must not let Miss Elizabeth slip away from me. While I do not ordinarily place significance on dreams, this one deeply moved me, and I immediately determined to come here when I awoke."

"Mr. Darcy," said Miss Elizabeth, "I had no idea you harbored such feelings for me. I had thought that you only looked on me with disgust—that I was not handsome enough to tempt a man of your standing."

"I regretted those words the moment they were spoken, Miss Bennet. As I have come to know you and as I have witnessed your lively nature and heard your spirited words and looked upon your dancing eyes, I have come to think of you as one of the handsomest— nay, as *the* handsomest woman of my acquaintance. Bingley's sisters attempted to convince me to go to London for the winter, but I could not do so, for I could not bear to leave your society. I thought at first that my feelings were naught but infatuation, but they have grown all the stronger, such that I cannot bear to let you go."

"Mr. Darcy," said Miss Elizabeth, "I should have expected you to marry the daughter of an earl or some heiress with lauded connections.

Are you certain that your interest in me is genuine?"

"I have never been so certain of anything in my life," said Mr. Darcy. "I confess I did once falter for reasons not unlike what you have described, but my love for you is strong enough that such concerns seem base and not worthy of consideration.

"If you were willing to marry Mr. Collins, then surely you can accept my suit in his stead. Please agree to marry me, Miss Bennet. I promise I shall do what I can to assist your mother and sisters when the time comes."

"I myself can argue no longer when faced with such an ardent suit," said Mr. Bennet, "but I suppose my arguments are not ultimately the most important. Lizzy, will you have Mr. Darcy?"

There was a pause, and then Miss Elizabeth finally spoke, the sound of her voice holding evidence of both laughter and tears. "I suppose I cannot argue with the ardency of such affections either. Yes, Mr. Darcy, I agree to be your wife."

"Miss Bennet," said Mr. Darcy, his words unmistakably joyful.

"I am glad to have my family's future secured in such a fashion," said Mr. Bennet. "Certainly, a load has been lifted from my shoulders. However, I must own that I actually am feeling as if I am a new man this morning. I shall not be surprised if I disappoint everyone and live."

Mr. Collins felt that this served as a fitting conclusion to the business to which he had needed to attend, and he smiled broadly as he stepped away from the door. He felt as if the spirit of Christmas had filled his very being to the brim with happiness. He had done quite well that day, and he praised himself for handling the situation so excellently.

Wanting to breathe in the fresh air of that Christmas morn one more time, he exited the house and raised his hands up to the sky, soaking in the rays of the brilliant sun beaming overhead. The day was perfect, and he would not change anything about it.

"Mr. Collins?" asked a voice in confusion.

He redirected his gaze and found Charlotte Lucas approaching and looking puzzled.

"Ah, Miss Lucas," said he warmly. "You appear to be quite surprised to see me. I suppose I might wonder whether you were coming to Longbourn this morning for the explicit purpose of being in my company."

"Actually," said Miss Lucas after a brief pause, "I was wondering why you were still in your nightclothes."

"Ah," said Mr. Collins, "I suppose that would seem rather odd." Then he hastened to excuse himself and return to his room to dress. Perhaps there was *one* thing he would have changed about that particular Christmas Day.

The End

FROM THE HEART

Colin Rowland

In the midst of an early Canadian snowstorm, I started to wonder about the same type of occurrence happening around Christmas when Mr. Darcy and Mr. Bingley have been called away on business. How might Elizabeth and Jane face the prospect of Christmas without their dearest loves?

℮lizabeth Bennet felt as if her spirits were sinking by the hour. Mr. Darcy had left for his estate of Pemberley on an unknown matter, and though she would never have expected her happiness to be so strongly affected by a temporary parting from a suitor, no matter how ardent her affections, she felt quite bereft. That he was gone was not out of the ordinary; the steward of his property, while competent and independent, on occasion deemed it necessary to request Mr. Darcy's presence to address an issue of one kind or another. During the few instances in which this had happened previously, Mr. Darcy had resolved the affair as fast as he was able and returned to Netherfield, often arriving in the wee hours of the morning, testament to his eagerness to see Elizabeth once more.

This trip, however, was unlike those taken previously, for the decision to travel was sudden. Mr. Darcy had invited Mr. Bingley along and departed hurriedly, leaving only a note written in haste and promising to return before Christmas should arrive.

To compound Elizabeth's anxiety, cold, wet weather had arrived soon after Mr. Darcy and Mr. Bingley commenced their travels, thereby causing her to suspend the morning walks she enjoyed each day. With little to occupy her, the usually good-natured young woman was gone, replaced by one who was quick-tempered and morose.

Elizabeth sat at the window, gazing toward the lane bordering the Longbourn estate. Her longing for her lover's company had manifested as an ache in her bosom which no attention to needlework or other pastimes could ease. Perhaps it was only natural that she should feel such a way due to the wondrous circumstances which had seemed to conspire in bringing the two of them together. From Mr. Darcy's slight at the spring assembly to his surprising reversal of feelings and ardent courtship, she could not help but confess to a feeling of thankfulness for her good fortune and the love she and Mr. Darcy shared.

"Lizzy," announced a voice from behind her. "Why so glum? Did not Mr. Darcy declare his intention to return with all urgency?"

"He did, Jane," said Elizabeth, "but I fear this inclement weather has caused a delay to those plans. The rain is falling heavily, and with it, the wind is strengthened. Furthermore, the lowering sky suggests the storm is not soon to be completed."

Jane peered through the window to the scene in the manor's yard. Though the drops of rain falling from the sky had begun the day small and light, they had now substantially grown in size and intensity, such that a curtain of water looked to have been drawn in front of the glass.

The wind had stepped up, with strong gusts fiercely driving the rain against the windowpane, as if attempting to gain access to the warmth of the room. Visibility for anyone outside in such a storm had been made difficult, if not impossible.

"I am sure Mr. Darcy intends to do whatever is in his power to return as soon as he is able," said Jane. "After all, Mr. Bingley is with him and will not allow unnecessary delay."

"I worry more that he shall make a rash decision to travel when it is unsafe to do so."

"Mr. Darcy is an uncommonly sensible man," said Jane. "I have no fear his own good sense will keep them safely at Pemberley until it is advisable to leave for Netherfield."

"What reason might have given adequate provocation to convince him a journey to his estate was vital in this season?" asked Elizabeth, her ire rising to the fore. "Furthermore, he left without a word of explanation!"

The sounds of children laughing and shouting with glee interrupted the exchange, as a pair of young girls ran through the sitting room, followed by an identical number of younger boys, seemingly intent upon catching their prey. The laughter which accompanied the youngsters was shrill and of a volume to overrule the possibility of speech.

"He would not have made such a decision on a mere whim," said Jane when the Gardiners' children had cleared the room. "Whatever the reason, I presume it was of sufficient urgency to urge his compliance. Let us go to the dining room. You may aid me in minding our young cousins, as they appear to be in a boisterous mood."

Taking her sister's hand, Jane drew her from the window and took her to the dining room, where a light midday meal had been prepared. The Gardiners' young brood had already been gathered for the meal; they giggled and teased one another as Mr. Gardiner attempted to encourage them to be seated.

"Elizabeth," said Mrs. Gardiner, "come enjoy the repast. It has been some time since last we visited, and I am given to understand you have caught the attention of an eligible suitor. Your mother is brimming with happiness and is speechless besides. I will rely on you to offer the details; for now, however, be seated, as we have much to review."

The Gardiners had come to Longbourn to spend the Christmas season, and while the estate ordinarily could not have been called a domicile of peace and quiet, now it was even further from matching such a description. Elizabeth would typically have relished the change, for she felt quite close to Mrs. Gardiner, but now her agitation kept her from properly enjoying the company.

Mrs. Gardiner appeared to have recognized the alteration in Elizabeth's mood, as she paused to search the young woman's downcast face for the smile she usually wore.

"Whatever is the problem, Lizzy?" asked she of her niece. "You bear an expression of unease. Is something amiss?"

"She is anxious for the safety of Mr. Darcy," said Jane. "He departed without notice for Pemberley three days ago, and his only communication was in the form of a brief note stating his intention of returning before Christmas Day. Lizzy fears that the worsening weather might delay his journey or that he will make a foolish choice to travel in defiance of the storm. It is my belief he is not the type to imperil himself or his companion without cause, but she is not to be persuaded."

"I am in agreement with Jane," said Mrs. Gardiner. "From the description I have been given, Mr. Darcy impresses me as a man in possession of an astute sense of propriety and a level head. He cannot be goaded into an unsafe judgment, no matter the depth of his desire to enjoy the pleasure of your company once again."

Elizabeth gave no reply, content to allow the discussion to end. In her heart, though, her anxiety continued, increasing each hour as the storm strengthened its assault on the manor and kept her bereft of the one whose proximity she most desired.

"Come," said Jane to Elizabeth when the meal was consumed. "Our cousins desire amusement, and I can see you are also in need of a distraction." Rising from her chair, she moved to the dining room door and waited for Elizabeth to join her. "We will play a game of Hoodman's Blind with them; this should capture their attention for the remainder of the day."

Elizabeth aided her sister in gathering the children and shepherding them into the sitting room, where the game was to be played. When they were seated, the fun began.

The afternoon was consumed in the playing of the game, with a new contest commencing each time one was completed. To her credit, Jane occupied Elizabeth in the amusement, so the latter's forebodings were swallowed up in her enjoyment of the games. When next the circumstances of Mr. Darcy's departure were recalled, the sun had set and the young cousins had been put to bed for the night.

"Thank you," said Elizabeth to Jane when the final child was tucked in and the last bedtime story related. "With your help, my focus transferred from petty issues to the joy of the children. Because of your ministrations, I have greatly enjoyed this day in spite of myself."

"Think nothing of it, dear sister," said Jane, "for you know I should do anything I can to alleviate your suffering."

Sounds arising from the sitting room brought the sisters to investigate. Entering, they found the room in the midst of a transformation. Mrs. Bennet and Mrs. Gardiner sat in chairs to either side of the fireplace, wherein roared a boisterous fire. Mrs. Bennet, comfortable in her favorite chair, directed her servants through vocalizations and broad gestures in the placement of boughs of greenery upon the tables and the fireplace mantle. Great branches of evergreen trees had been harvested and set above, below, and to either side of the room's windows, and the fragrant aroma of the freshly cut greenery added to the excitement of the approaching holiday. Kitty and Lydia busied themselves with the setting of candles at the sides of the boughs in readiness for the commencement of the Christmas observance to begin on the morrow. Above the entrances and over many of the rooms in the manor hung kissing boughs of mistletoe, with twigs of berries lining each sprig. Strings of gaily colored paper dangled from each corner of the room, crossing in the center and continuing to the opposite corners.

"How festive is the transformation of Longbourn!" said Jane in appreciation of the change wrought. "As always, my anticipation of Christmastime is equaled and even surpassed by the artistry of the decorations displayed throughout the manor, but especially in this room. This gives expression to Christmas and typifies the spirit prevalent at this time of the year.

"Of course, I most look forward to attending tomorrow's morning service. The holly and ivy adorning the entrance to the chapel are always exquisite to behold. Furthermore, I find the Christmas sermon to be my favorite of the year."

"As long as the vicar does not include mention of that infernal Fordyce," declared Mr. Bennet, who had entered the room behind Jane, "I will be content. I shall never understand why he insists upon frequent references to that charlatan in defiance of my injunction to the contrary."

"Now, Papa," said Elizabeth, "allow him this instance of disobedience without reprimand. You must look upon his freedom to form his sermon in the manner he wishes as a symbol of the gift we have all been given and commemorate on this day more than at any other time. This, after all, is the reason for our celebration, is it not?"

Mr. Bennet grunted, though Elizabeth could not be sure whether it was in agreement, and after surveying the room, he declared the decorations acceptable before returning to his library and the solitude of his many tomes.

Elizabeth approached the window again to peer through its panes, now frosted by the frigid north wind blowing the rainfall at the house with ever increasing strength. The storm's ferocity had doubled, with the torrent now appearing to be driven sideways by a wind freshened to the force of a gale. In an instant, her sense of unease returned, and with it came renewed fear for the welfare of the travelers whom she and her sister awaited.

"It looks as if this inclement weather has become less amenable to those foolish enough to be out of doors," said Jane, who had stepped to Elizabeth's side to gaze through the window's panes, which were now rattling with each fresh gust of wind. "I should not think to see Mr. Bingley and Mr. Darcy arrive tonight, as they will have sought rooms in which to wait for the elements to calm somewhat before setting out anew. Mr. Darcy must no doubt have concluded it folly to continue their journey in weather of this nature."

"I pray your supposition is correct," said Elizabeth. "I would much prefer that he conclude his journey uninjured two days hence than to know I was the cause of a foolish bid to effect a speedy return at such a time when the prudent course is for an exercise of patience." Still, despite her statements to the contrary, in Elizabeth's heart nestled the desire for his arrival to take place before the night was concluded.

In vain, she remained by the window, hoping to serve as witness to the triumphal entrance of the two travelers. To quell her growing distress, she recommenced working on a piece of embroidery she had discarded earlier in the day. Her progress was halting, with numerous stoppages caused by her penchant for introspection as thoughts of Mr. Darcy arose unbidden with ever-increasing regularity. At last, as her eyes began to close of their own accord, she set the needlework aside and took herself to her bed, where, with a silent prayer for the eventual arrival of the two gentlemen, she closed her eyes.

Elizabeth was the first to rise the next morning, as was her custom. Donning her dressing gown, she stepped to her bedchamber window, where the sight which greeted her was of a world shrouded in a blanket of white, the rain having changed to snow that fell in fat, lazy flakes, although at an intensity sharply reduced from the deluge of the previous day. Gone too was the fearsome wind; having laid an effective claim to its supremacy, it had dissipated, stealing away like a thief in the night.

With haste born of her anxiety and impatience, Elizabeth dressed and bustled down the stairs to the manor entrance. Throwing open the immense door, she surveyed the perfect scene before her of a landscape painted in white, thus far unmarred by the print of man or beast.

"Is there a sign of their arrival?" asked Jane, who waited at the foot of the staircase, concern etched upon her brow.

"I see only undisturbed snow," said Elizabeth. "I presume they are delayed by last evening's poor weather. If so, I do not expect them to reach Hertfordshire before tomorrow.

"Now, come, Jane. Let us prepare for the Christmas services at church." Elizabeth shooed her sister away from the entrance and to the dining room, where Mrs. Hill had laid out a hearty breakfast in preparation for their yule observance.

The meal became a family affair, as each member, upon learning it was prepared, came downstairs to partake of the sumptuous fare. The conversation was muted, as each of the Bennets found more interest in the appetizing offerings than in entertaining a discussion of any substance.

"The time has come to prepare for the vicar's Christmas sermon," said Mr. Bennet once he finally rose from the table to conclude the meal. "We will leave for the parish in one hour; your participation, as you know, is required." This last was directed to Lydia and Kitty, both of whom were unapologetically resistant to the idea of church attendance on such a day.

Elizabeth, wanting to arrive at the chapel early, extended what aid she could in hastening the preparations of her two youngest sisters, over their strenuous objections. In short order, all were ready to depart, and the Bennet carriage was brought to the door, accompanied by the landau which had carried the Gardiners from London. Once arguments about seating arrangements had been settled and assigned positions assumed, the carriages departed Longbourn village for the short ride to the church.

When first she alit from the transport, Elizabeth was equal parts surprised and pleased to discover Mr. Darcy waiting for her with Mr. Bingley at his side. Standing apart from the men was Mr. Darcy's sister, Georgiana. Delighted by their safe return, Elizabeth hurried, as much as proper decorum would allow, to greet them.

"It is a relief to find you in attendance, but more especially to see that you seem safe and well," said she when near enough to speak without needing to raise her voice. "I was concerned that you and Mr. Bingley had pressed on in spite of the weather, and I feared some harm may have reached you."

"We were fortunate," said Mr. Darcy, "in that we did not encounter foul weather until we had neared the environs of Hertfordshire. The final leg of the journey was somewhat perilous, but the majority of our travel was conducted in relative comfort. For this, I am thankful, as my sister made the choice to come with us on our return to Netherfield, and I could not deny her wish to spend Christmas Day together."

Elizabeth turned to Georgiana and gathered the girl into her arms, encasing her in a brief and welcoming hug. "Georgiana, it is so good to see you again," said she, "and on this most precious of holidays besides. I look forward to sharing the latest news with you after the service and hope you will do the same with me."

Lowering her voice so only Georgiana could hear, she added: "Mr. Darcy has informed me of the posting of that scoundrel Wickham to the Scottish border. I am so glad he will not be allowed to bother you again."

Elizabeth released her friend and stepped back to regard Mr. Darcy. "Miss Darcy is fortunate, indeed, to have a brother so devoted. I commend the love and devotion you have shown in affording her the comfort and companionship of her only family at this special time."

Elizabeth glanced around briefly. "But what of Miss Bingley and Mr. and Mrs. Hurst? Did they remain at Netherfield this morning?"

"Caroline wished to celebrate Christmastide in London," said Mr. Bingley. "She was able to persuade Mr. and Mrs. Hurst to accompany her, as they also wished to return to the city." Leaning close to Elizabeth, he said in a voice so soft it was barely above a whisper's volume: "I guess they are not as enamored of Hertfordshire as Mr. Darcy and I are."

Before she could offer a reply, Mr. Bennet bade the party enter the chapel for the Christmas observance. Mr. Darcy offered one arm to Elizabeth and the other to his sister, and together, they joined those already seated in anticipation of the yule liturgy.

Elizabeth's enjoyment of the ceremony was curtailed by the irreverence of the two youngest Bennets, whose carryings-on were noted by most of those close to them. Of necessity, she was called upon to quiet their whispers and calm the fidgeting mannerisms with which each girl was infected, to no avail. In a final act born of desperation, she separated the two, placing Lydia beside Mr. Darcy and Kitty next to herself; in so doing, she was at last able to turn her attention to the parson, who by this time had nearly finished his exhortations.

The saving grace, to Elizabeth at least, was the unchanging nature of his Christmas service; this vicar, who had assumed the living twelve years before, delivered the same lesson each year, with nary a word amended. While her preference was to give the parson's words her full attention, the peaceful and joyous feeling this Christmas encouraged in her heart was ample reward for her attendance.

"Will you and the rest of the Netherfield party join us in our celebration at Longbourn?" asked Mr. Bennet as they filed from the chapel at the conclusion of the service.

"We do not wish to intrude," said Mr. Darcy. "This is a time to spend with family and those whom we love; I fear our presence could detract from your appreciation of one another."

"Take no thought to the matter," replied Mr. Bennet. "I know my two eldest daughters will enjoy the company, and to be truthful, I will as well, as it gives me the joy of conducting a conversation with someone not of the female persuasion."

"I would be honored," said Mr. Darcy, "and I can with confidence accept for Mr. Bingley. Am I correct in assuming your overture includes my sister?"

"You have no need to ask," said Mr. Bennet. "I cannot presume to exclude a member of your family, especially one who is a friend of my Lizzy."

"Then it is settled," declared Mr. Darcy. "We will make our way to Longbourn within the hour."

As promised, the guests arrived before the expiration of the hour in a grand coach, which stopped to disgorge Georgiana before continuing around to the kitchen entrance, where Mr. Darcy and Mr. Bingley stepped from the vehicle. Mr. Darcy summoned a stablehand and exchanged a few quiet words with him, whereupon he and Mr. Bingley returned to the main entrance. Then, in the company of Georgiana, they entered the manor.

"Welcome to Longbourn once again," greeted Mr. Bennet, who had been waiting for their arrival, which only spoke to his eagerness for more varied company. "Did you encounter a problem with your transport? I saw you chose not to stop, but rather continued around to the rear of the manor."

"I requested aid on an issue from the boy who was summoned to tend the horses," said Mr. Darcy. "It is of minor importance and will be resolved before we take our leave tonight."

"I see," said Mr. Bennet. "I hope it causes no significant problem. I suppose we might now join the company of those in the sitting room." Turning, he led the party along the hall to a room where sounds of lively discussions merged with the noises of children at play, the effect being a joyous mixture of incongruous harmony.

Into this bedlam, Mr. Bennet led the newly arrived visitors. Their entrance caused a cessation of the noise for a brief moment before it resumed once again.

The two gentlemen, accompanied by Miss Darcy, greeted Mrs. Bennet before seeking permission from Jane and Elizabeth to sit with them, a request which was granted without delay. As the men seated themselves, Lydia and Kitty, in what for them was an unusual bit of welcoming behavior, invited Georgiana to join them in their amusements.

They passed most of the afternoon in this manner until Mrs. Hill appeared and beckoned for Mr. Darcy to join her in conversation, to the apparent confusion of Jane and Elizabeth and the seeming amusement of Mr. Bingley. A few words were exchanged, and Mr. Darcy disappeared from view, causing further bewilderment, particularly with regard to the more vocal Mrs. Bennet and Mrs. Philips. After fifteen minutes had elapsed, Mr. Darcy still had not reappeared, and Mrs. Bennet could no longer contain her curiosity.

"Has a problem arisen with Mr. Darcy's carriage?" asked Mrs. Bennet. "If so, why was Mrs. Hill sent to inform him?" When an answer was not offered, she laid her hand upon the bell and rang it once to summon her maid. The bell's peal was answered by Mr. Darcy, who stepped to the door clad in a cooking apron, to the astonishment of all but Mr. Bingley, who stepped forward to join him, donning an apron Mr. Darcy extended to him, an act that caused smiles to break forth on the faces of many in attendance.

Attention now turned to Mr. Darcy, whose own face was wreathed in a smile of complete joy. "I drove my carriage to the kitchen door so as to provide Mrs. Hill with six Christmas turkeys I had purchased and brought for this occasion," said he. "I spoke with your dear servant and instructed her to prepare them for the Christmas meal, and she has now finished doing so."

"This is much more than we will consume," said Mrs. Bennet. "I thank you for the generosity you have shown, but I am afraid we will need to dispose of a great part of this magnificent repast when it is not eaten."

"Fear not," said Mr. Darcy. "My intention is to show my appreciation for those who have served without complaint this past year. My instructions to Mrs. Hill were to see to the preparation of these six fowl. Two of the birds are set aside for the occupants of this manor, but the others have been sent to those residents of Longbourn who are not as fortunate. They are at present enjoying a feast comparable to our own; Mr. Bingley and I have donned these aprons to act as servers for this banquet so that the house staff may join the festivities with the rest of your tenants and servants. This was a tradition established long ago by my own father, and it is one I have carried on in his stead.

"Now, if you please, I would request your presence at the table, where your Christmas meal awaits."

Miss Elizabeth sat unmoving as everyone repaired to the other room to seat themselves for their feast. Darcy, noting her lack of movement, came up beside her where she sat at the fire, gazing into the flames.

"Will you not join your family in partaking of the meal?" asked Darcy with concern born of love. "Or has a mistake on my part brought sorrow to you?"

Miss Elizabeth looked up at him, her eyes brimming with tears. "Your gesture has overwhelmed me, Mr. Darcy. Never have I been witness to such a display of love and charity for others."

Darcy beheld the young woman, his heart overfull with the love which had blossomed in him throughout the past several months. Her visible emotion touched him, and in that instant, he came to the conclusion there was no other for him. In a moment he would forever recall with tenderness, he dropped to a knee and took her hand in his. Nearly overcome with emotion, he brought the hand to his lips to brush it lightly with a kiss.

"Miss Bennet," said he with a voice grown husky with fervor, "you are the only one for me. You occupy my waking hours and fill my dreams with your presence when I try, unsuccessfully, to find sleep. I can envision no future without you to share it beside me. Please accept this offer of marriage and allow me to reclaim even a small portion of the sanity I have sacrificed in my preoccupation with you."

"How shall I answer?" responded Miss Elizabeth, her words inspiring fear to invade Mr. Darcy's heart and threaten his composure. "I, too, have experienced profound growth in the level of my feelings toward you. I have entertained thoughts of our life together should you offer and have been sure of my response."

Darcy felt dread and the expectation of her refusal of his proposal. Near desperation, he opened his mouth to commence a final effort to convince her of the advantages that would be hers should she agree to wed him. His words, however, were stopped before they could be uttered, as Elizabeth began again to speak.

"I will be the happiest, proudest, and most sublime creature ever to exist upon becoming the wife of Mr. Fitzwilliam Darcy."

Darcy remained still for a moment, unsure of his correct interpretation of her statement until he brought his gaze to fasten upon her face. The joy which shone in her eyes soon relieved his trepidation, and murmuring her name, he grasped her hand to press a kiss upon it.

Springing to his feet, Darcy led her to the dining room and the company of her family. Mr. Bennet, upon witnessing their entrance, looked at Darcy and gave a nod that the latter took as affirmation of his approval of their intended union. Darcy had never been happier than he felt in that moment.

Elizabeth, ever careful of her mother's feelings and mortified in her presumption of the reaction that the news of her engagement might provoke in the woman, waited until night arrived and their guests departed before she informed Mrs. Bennet of what her father had known for most of the evening hours.

At mid-morning the next day, Elizabeth witnessed the arrival of Mr. Darcy in a carriage of grander size than the one he had ridden the day before. With him was Mr. Bingley, looking for all the world as one who wished to have remained within the warmth of his sheets. Stepping to the window, she observed as Mr. Darcy and his friend made their way to the Longbourn tenants' homes, their arms laden with boxes. An hour and a half passed before she next spied them, trudging through the unmelted snow to the manor. In haste, she tidied her hair and waited in the sitting room to greet them.

"A rewarding beginning to the day," was Mr. Darcy's statement to Mr. Bingley as they entered the room.

"Where might this reward be found?" asked Elizabeth.

"Mr. Bingley was my company on a mission to present the good residents of Longbourn with gifts of aid and esteem," answered Mr. Darcy. "This is the second part of my father's legacy which I have continued since his passing. It is my intention to bestow the same affection upon Pemberley's tenants when I return to my estate next week. It is my hope you will join me in the continuation of this tradition as Mistress of Pemberley."

"I would like nothing more," said Elizabeth, her heart singing with warmth and affection toward this generous man. She would be honored to soon join him as his wife, and she would gladly undertake all the duties that assumption of the post of Pemberley's mistress entailed.

"I have received a letter from my cousin, Mr. Collins," said Mr. Bennet a few minutes later as he stepped into the room, "wherein he relates his disappointment at his inability to observe Christmastide with us, as he was occupied by his responsibilities at Rosings Park. He sends his regrets and wishes all a joyous celebration. Mr. Collins completes the missive with a promise to visit us sometime in the new year."

Mr. Bennet crumpled the sheet and, stepping to the hearth, placed it upon the fire, where it was soon consumed.

"It is my wish," said he, "that his patroness might find herself in need of Mr. Collins's services much more frequently in the new year than she has in the past."

"Perhaps, Papa," said Elizabeth with a look of innocence directed toward Mr. Darcy, "we can entice an acquaintance to assist with the success of your ambition."

"Please accept my apology," said Mr. Darcy with a smile, "but I am possessed of no desire to infuriate my aunt by suggesting something of this nature. Having met the man, I am of the opinion she will find herself in need of respite from her vicar, and I cannot deny her such relief. You, as his closest relation, should welcome the man's attention."

The laughter which greeted his statement was shared by all and became the impetus for the establishment of close bonds between Mr. Bennet and his future sons-in-law on that Christmas Day.

The End

TRADITIONS OF CHRISTMAS

Jann Rowland

The other side of the coin of the challenge Lelia mentions with regard to her A Christmas Gift story. When I wrote this several years ago, I based it on the world of my first novel, Acting on Faith. When I dusted it off for this anthology, I repurposed it to happen in a random world so that those reading it will not be lost at sea with references to that work. As Lelia suggested, my writing has changed quite a bit over the years. But I still enjoy this brief look into the lives of our favorite couple.

*E*lizabeth watched dubiously as her betrothed knelt in front of her, fastening a pair of ice skates to her boots. "Are you certain about this, William?"

"What?" exclaimed William, a look of mock astonishment on his features. "The intrepid Miss Elizabeth Bennet cannot find her way around a small pond on a pair of skates?"

"Your mood is entirely too ebullient, sir," accused Elizabeth.

"It is not every day that I am allowed to teach you something new, my dear," replied William as he gave one of the skates a tug to tighten the straps. "You are far too independent; I relish the chance to be with you as you try something new."

"But skates?" persisted Elizabeth "Shall we not instead try an activity that does not involve strapping something to my feet which shall only make the ice even slipperier?"

Elizabeth knew very well that she sounded petulant, but she was enjoying provoking her betrothed. William was a dear man who provided for her every comfort and need whenever he was able, but he was taking far too much pleasure in the fact that she had never been ice-skating before. She suspected his state of mind was primarily because of his astonishment that an outdoor activity existed which she had not previously tried.

"Is she still complaining?" interrupted Anne de Bourgh as she glided up to them. She executed a pirouette in coming to a stop at the edge of the pond and then stood smiling down at Elizabeth with amusement.

"Speaking of ebullience," groused Elizabeth with a glower, "I am afraid your cousin appears to have caught your mood, William."

Anne only smiled at her, and Elizabeth could tell that she was suppressing her mirth with some effort, though it was a near thing. Anne's arrival—without her mother—had been a great surprise to all, though Miss Bingley had rallied to use the woman's appearance to her own advantage. At least, she *attempted* to do so—Miss Bingley had not been happy when Anne had expressed an eagerness to meet Elizabeth as her main reason for coming.

"I still cannot fathom how *you*, of all people, know how to ice skate," said Elizabeth. "Should your lady mother, 'excessively attentive' as she is to all of your concerns in general and your bodily health in particular, not have prohibited you from learning? I was not aware that ice was a part of Kent's landscape. Is it not the garden of the kingdom?"

"It is, though that does not mean that we do not have winter, as you well know," replied Anne, her amusement unflagging. "Besides, I have not always been ill, and certainly have never been as unhealthy as my mother imagines. As a young girl, I played as any young girl would, though my mother was still very protective of me. As I grew older, there were, I will confess, some instances in which my dear cousins would sneak me out to the pond at Pemberley for a little ice skating while my aunts and uncles occupied my mother."

At this piece of intelligence, Elizabeth turned to her fiancé and regarded him with an astonished air. "Did I hear you correctly, Miss de Bourgh? The great and ever-proper Mr. Darcy actually condescended to *sneak*?"

"I have been known to do my fair share of sneaking," was William's mild reply.

Unconvinced, Elizabeth regarded him, knowing very well that he was not as stiff as she had first thought him to be. Since their engagement, William had shown even more of a playful side to his character—especially where Elizabeth was concerned—than she had thought existed. Of course, it was up to her to provoke it wherever possible, as she adored seeing a smile on his countenance. Not that a smile was now a rare occurrence—his relations had commented many times on the effect his relationship with her had wrought on him. He had not had much reason to smile since his father's passing.

"Is Miss Bennet still reluctant to come on the ice?" said Colonel Fitzwilliam as he skated up to them and executed a sudden stop, sending ice crystals showering through the air. With him was Georgiana, who glided atop the pond with little apparent effort, as though she had been born with a pair of skates attached to her feet. The pair had arrived at Netherfield some days earlier at Mr. Bingley's invitation to spend Christmastide with them all. Given the opportunity to come to know Georgiana better after their interactions that summer was a blessing, as the girl had proven to be everything a future sister should be.

Elizabeth's eyes narrowed as she stared at Colonel Fitzwilliam, expressing her displeasure at his too jovial tone. For that matter, her sisters, who followed behind the Colonel, were showing a disturbing proficiency on the ice. She knew that Lydia and Kitty had at times visited the pond, though she had not known just how skilled they were at traversing across it. In hindsight, she wished they would have spent even more time ice-skating, as it was one of the only activities they indulged in that did not involve redcoats, flirting, or exposing themselves to all and sundry. Even Mary, Elizabeth noticed, was showing a competence, if not a flair, that was unexpected.

"You are looking at this in the wrong fashion, Miss Bennet," said the Colonel with a twinkle in his eye. Elizabeth by now knew the man well enough to discern that such an expression meant trouble. Unfortunately, she was correct.

"This is an opportunity to be in the arms of your betrothed before you are married."

The tinkling of Anne's laughter filled the small clearing, echoed by the Colonel's guffaw and Kitty's giggle. Georgiana, too, was smiling, though a laugh did not escape her lips, and Mary appeared to be scandalized.

William, however, dear man that he was, glanced up at the Colonel with promised retribution in his eyes.

"Ah, I can see the besotted and protective suitor has appeared," said Colonel Fitzwilliam, though he was not intimidated in the least. "Then I shall leave you to it.

"Come, Anne," continued the Colonel, taking his cousin's arm. "Let us leave the lovers to their own devices."

They turned away and began to skate across the pond, followed by Mary and Kitty. Georgiana, however, glided forward and favored Elizabeth with a smile.

"You will learn quickly, Elizabeth," said she. "William is a very good instructor, and I know that you can do anything you attempt."

Elizabeth returned the girl's smile with eager warmth. "Then how could I refuse? I shall not disappoint you, Georgiana."

"I doubt that is even possible," said Georgiana.

Then Elizabeth, feeling playful, said: "Though I have neither genius nor taste when it pertains to skating, I am certain that my vanity will give me application. But I do not doubt that it will likewise give me a pedantic air and conceited manner which would injure a higher degree of excellence than I am capable of reaching."

Georgiana and William laughed at her words.

"Oh, Lizzy!" exclaimed Georgiana with some enthusiasm. "I shall love to have you for a sister!"

Upon seeing the young girl's sudden look of embarrassment at her outburst, Elizabeth hastened to assure her: "As I will love having *you* for a sister, Georgie."

Smiling with delight, Georgiana turned and, after admonishing William to teach Elizabeth properly, skated away.

"Shall we?" asked William as he stood and extended his hand.

Nodding, Elizabeth pushed herself up off her seat, grateful that the snow at the edge of the pond was soft enough that her skates sunk into it and provided her with a little stability and balance. It would not do to fall on her behind before she even made it to the ice!

"Come, Elizabeth," said her suitor, his reassurance warming her. "I shall guide you and will not allow you to fall."

Though she said nothing in response, Elizabeth followed him the few steps to the ice; then, after he had stepped out onto the hard surface himself, she followed him and put her own foot on the ice.

And of course, she promptly had it slide out from under her. She clung to William for dear life as he performed his office and supported her while she tried to gain her balance.

"I am certain you have already apprehended this, my dear," said William, "but standing on skates differs greatly from standing on your boots."

"Do tell," was Elizabeth's dry reply. She managed to straighten herself and stand on the blades, and she soon felt that she would be well as long as she did not attempt to move.

"Indeed," said William, ignoring her sarcasm. "Walking on skates is possible, but it must be done slowly. You must be much more careful about how you move. If you move as though you were walking on a tiled floor, you are liable to fall."

He moved away from her, leaving her standing at the side of the pond. "When you wish to move, you must use the sharpness of the blade to gain purchase enough to push off. Like this."

He dug the blade of his left skate into the ice and pushed, gliding with effortless grace away from her. He pushed off several more times, turning and gliding toward her and then stopping in front of her much as the Colonel had, but with much less exuberance.

"I doubt I shall be able to stop in such a manner," said Elizabeth.

"Stopping does take much more practice," answered he. "But I shall stay with you, so you shall not be required to stop by yourself today.

"Now, come; let us go."

Stepping to her side, William put a hand around her waist and grasped her by the arm; together, they pushed off and began to skate across the pond. At first, Elizabeth did not do much—she allowed her fiancé to propel them forward, gliding along with him at his guidance. But as they continued, being the intrepid woman that she was, she started to move with him, and she slowly began to become accustomed to the motions of skating, though she well knew that she would not become proficient at once.

As she became accustomed to what she was doing, she was able to pay a little more attention to her surroundings. The pond on which they skated was situated at the very back of Longbourn's property, in a maze of wilderness that only those familiar with the area could find.

Though Elizabeth rarely came here, the scene at present was idyllic. A blanket of white snow covered the area, the result of a heavy fall only the night before, and the white coating decorated the trees with its sparkling brilliance. Even those trees bereft of their summer mantle appeared somehow majestic and beautiful despite the fact that they were sleeping out the winter. The boughs of the evergreen trees were also heavy with the white powder, lending them a festive air, much as the decorated trees of which Elizabeth had heard tales in the past.

"Elizabeth!" cried Anne as she skated up to them. "I see that you are becoming accustomed to the ice!"

"I must practice much more if I am ever to be accepted as being an accomplished ice-skater by your lady mother," replied Elizabeth with a laugh.

"Oh, but my mother does not skate," said Anne. "Of course, if she had, then she would be a true proficient, you know."

They laughed together at Anne's imitation of her mother while William looked on with an indulgent smile.

"When you *have* become proficient," continued Anne after a moment, "you *must* join us in a game of tag."

"But if I do that, then I shall be required to catch one of you, which I shall never succeed in doing. I think I will instead be content to skate with William."

"Then I shall leave you to it," said Anne with a laugh before she once again skated away.

A few minutes later, William prodded: "Are you looking forward to Christmas?"

"I am," said Elizabeth with a smile. "It is my favorite time of the year. And you shall certainly see how the Bennet family celebrates the season."

"I am anticipating it greatly, I assure you," replied William. "Though Georgiana and I have spent Christmas with the Matlocks a few times, some years we have had only each other for company. A large gathering with many friends is a welcome change."

Elizabeth looked on him with feigned astonishment. "Mr. Fitzwilliam Darcy, a man who hates large gatherings, is actually looking forward to Christmas with my voluble mother?"

"There will be many others in attendance apart from your mother," said William, his features betraying his amusement. "After all, am I not now her favorite future son-in-law?"

"You are her *only* future son-in-law, now that Jane and Mr. Bingley are married," pointed out Elizabeth.

"This only ensures the firmness of my position."

He was being entirely too smug, Elizabeth thought, but she decided to allow it to pass.

Instead of trying to chip away at that smugness, she asked: "Are you looking forward to Mr. Bingley's return?"

His amusement faded in a grimace. "I am," said he. "The Hursts are at Netherfield already, I am afraid. As you know, Hurst is not the most interesting conversationalist, and Mrs. Hurst is not much better. Then add to the mix Miss Bingley's determination to prove to me I have made a mistake in offering for you, and it equals a most uncomfortable situation."

"Oh, you poor dear," said Elizabeth with a laugh. "Do you need me to save you from the big, bad Miss Bingley?"

William laughed. "I believe I shall manage, Elizabeth."

Elizabeth laughed along with him before she asked him another question. "So what shall I expect Christmastide to be like as Mrs. Darcy? Do you have any traditions passed down from your parents that you wish to continue?"

"Whatever traditions you bring with you should suffice, my dear."

"I will be most happy to share," said Elizabeth. "But you must have some traditions of your own."

"We do," confirmed William. "We decorate the house with festive candles, boughs of holly, and all manner of ribbons and other trimmings of the season. The most prominent of our traditions, however, is our Christmas tree."

Elizabeth turned to him with some surprise. "You decorate a tree?"

"In actuality, we have not had a tree since my mother died." His countenance had turned pensive with introspection. "She always insisted upon having a Christmas tree decorated with ribbons, nuts, fruits, and candles every year."

"Was she not ahead of her time?" asked Elizabeth curiously. "I had understood that Queen Charlotte had introduced the practice to England only ten years ago."

"And it still has not truly been accepted, except by certain members of the highest circles," agreed William. "But the custom is much older in certain areas in Germany. My mother visited some distant relations in that country when she was a girl, and she was so enamored of the custom that she insisted upon it when she returned. Her father indulged her, and the Fitzwilliams have decorated a tree at Christmas ever since. My mother brought the custom with her when she married my father.

"But with my mother's death, my father could not bear to carry on the tradition. Though we still observed the season and performed some of the more traditional customs, our Christmases became much less prominent after that."

Throughout the course of his narrative, William's voice had changed from introspective to wistful, leaving Elizabeth to wish that she had not provoked such painful memories.

In an attempt to restore his former good spirits, she responded: "Then we shall have to continue the custom, assuming it is not too painful for you."

William turned and gazed at her, and she fancied she could see his heart in his eyes. "I believe that I shall be eager to experience the happiness I felt with my mother once more. The resumption of that particular tradition could never bring pain, especially if I share it with you."

"I will do whatever it takes to make you happy," replied Elizabeth with a smile, "for I love you so very dearly."

"And I love you," replied her betrothed.

They skated in silence for several more moments, each basking in the warmth of love and the companionship of the other. Elizabeth gazed about the pond, watching her sisters skate with the Colonel, Anne, and Georgiana. This was what Christmas was about, she decided. The close ties of family, the observance of the Savior's birth, and the hope of peace throughout the land. This year would be the first of many such wonderful times spent together with these wonderful people, and she could not be happier.

"Perhaps we could persuade my mother to place a tree in our parlor," suggested Elizabeth. "I would love to begin our traditions together this year instead of waiting until next."

"I am certain she will allow us to do so, my dearest Elizabeth," replied Mr. Darcy. "After all, I *am* her favorite son-in-law-to-be, am I not?"

Elizabeth simply laughed.

The End

THE MATCHMAKING SCHEMES OF ANNE DE BOURGH

Lelia Eye

Anne is a character with a lot of potential. We see her as sick and weak in Pride and Prejudice, *but if that problem is taken away, then it seems she might have at least a little of her mother's officiousness in her. Of course, her attempts at interference are much more pleasant to face than her mother's.*

*A*nne de Bourgh loved the smell of Christmastide.

The decorations of fir, rosemary, yew, and sundry evergreens all combined to create a comforting smell that filled Anne's heart with gladness. For years, her sickness of body had forced her to experience the outdoors from a distance through the use of her phaeton, and she always greatly anticipated the opportunity to be surrounded by such ornamentation as tree boughs, ivy garlands, and holly sprigs during the Christmas season. During those times, she could easily imagine herself walking through a forest, touching plants here and there with the fondness of a mother being reunited with children from whom she had long been parted.

A few years ago, however, her life began to change for the better. Anne's cousin, Fitzwilliam Darcy, had located a promising young doctor who was not mired in traditional methods and who was willing to experiment with different approaches. Anne's mother, Lady Catherine de Bourgh, had grumbled about Darcy's interference, but she had agreed to allow the doctor an opportunity to treat Anne. That had turned out to be the greatest blessing of Anne's life.

The doctor's care and guidance slowly breathed life into Anne's frail body; anyone who saw her would have sworn she was a new person entirely within a year of receiving treatments. It had taken some time for Lady Catherine to own that her daughter had improved, but she had finally done so, and now Anne had been given the opportunity to spend Christmas at Darcy's townhouse in London. She felt grateful beyond measure for all that her cousin had done for her, but she was at a loss as to how she could repay him. At least, she felt that way until an introduction to the Bennet family revealed that Darcy seemed to have a particular interest in a delightful young woman called Elizabeth Bennet.

As one who had been ill of body for some time, Anne had grown accustomed to observing others closely in lieu of expending energy conversing with them. It had not taken long to see how often Darcy's eyes fell on Miss Elizabeth. Of course, even had she missed the obvious signs, she could not have failed to see how eagerly Darcy introduced his sister to the young woman. Still, after Miss Elizabeth and her family departed, Anne made certain to find a way to speak to her cousin alone so that she might fully gauge his attachment.

"Did you spend much time in company with the Bennet family in Hertfordshire?" asked Anne, her tone nonchalant.

"Indeed. Bingley has been courting Miss Bennet, so our calls at Longbourn were quite frequent."

Having seen Mr. Bingley's behavior in company with Jane Bennet, Anne was unsurprised. "He must have been glad to learn they would spend Christmas with their relations in town, for that meant your plans and theirs aligned quite well."

"Certainly, he was."

From the Bennets' recent visit, Anne understood that Mr. Bennet had come to London well in advance of the rest of his family on some urgent business, and judging by the affection evident between Mr. Bingley and Miss Bennet, she wondered whether the pair could have become secretly engaged in Hertfordshire and had only been waiting for an opportunity to gain Mr. Bennet's approval. Still, regardless of the extent of the couple's affections, she thought her cousin had taken Mr. Bingley's and Miss Bennet's interest in each other rather well.

"I am surprised you have not encouraged Mr. Bingley to make a better match," said Anne. "After all, I understand from my mother that the dowries of Mr. Bennet's daughters are not much of which to speak."

"Bingley has money enough for his purposes. A greater consideration for a man of his character should be his feelings for his future bride. She is the daughter of a gentleman, so he need not look elsewhere as long as her feelings match his own."

"Should not love be the greatest consideration for most men looking to marry?"

"Certainly not," said Darcy.

"What about you, Cousin?"

"I beg your pardon?"

"Do you intend for love to be a factor in your choice of a bride? You have money enough and connections enough, so you have been afforded a great deal of freedom that many young men lack. I know we had decided long ago that we would not suit, but have you given consideration to someone who might?"

Her cousin remained quiet, either mulling over the response to her question or trying to decide whether to answer.

"I suspect you may already have someone whose affections you wish to gain," said Anne, probing further.

Darcy looked at her for a few moments, scrutinizing her. "I do not believe I have ever seen your meddling side before. Perhaps something of your mother's character has been passed down to you after all."

Anne smiled. "If you wish to keep your cards hidden, then so be it. I shall simply find a different way to obtain the information I want."

Then she left him before he could inquire as to what precisely she meant.

It took some prodding before Lady Catherine finally conceded to host a dinner party. As Georgiana was too young to serve as hostess and Miss Bingley had left with the Hursts to stay with Mr. Hurst's family, the task fell to Lady Catherine. Anne attempted to volunteer to serve as hostess herself, but Lady Catherine had declared the position to be too strenuous for Anne to undertake. Darcy was easily convinced of the pleasure to be had in such a party by Anne, though she suspected that might have been because a good portion of her guest list was comprised of the Bennets and Gardiners.

The late Lady Anne had enjoyed hosting dinner parties, so the Darcy townhouse was more than equipped to host a large number of guests. Fortunately, while notice of the party was of necessity short, all of the guests invited agreed to attend.

Darcy's cook and housekeeper had both been none too pleased with the short notice, but they had proven themselves capable of meeting the challenge with the addition of some temporary staff, and five days after Christmas found the party seated at a splendid feast. Savory mince pies, bright green florets of broccoli, glistening apple and pear preserves, steaming roast beef, rich plum pudding, several types of seasonal fish and prawns, wild boar, and a variety of other dishes served to tempt the hungry.

Anne had, through a series of maneuvers, succeeded in ensuring Darcy and Miss Elizabeth were seated next to each other, and now, from her place across the table and a few seats down, she waited and listened, attempting to determine whether there was any evidence of the sparks of romance flying.

"I can scarcely recall the last time I saw a feast such as this," said Miss Elizabeth to Darcy. "I do not believe I have ever even seen such a spread on Christmas Day itself."

"My aunt and cousin have outdone themselves," responded the gentleman. "My cousin has not been to London since she was quite young due to a chronic illness that she has finally overcome, so I suspect the excitement of novelty has had some part to play in it."

"This is to be a celebration, then," said Miss Elizabeth with a smile.

"I suppose you could call it such," said Darcy, dipping his head.

When Anne looked at the slight smile that tugged at the corners of her cousin's mouth, she became convinced that her cousin was close to falling in love with Elizabeth Bennet.

As she watched, she noticed Miss Elizabeth struggling to cut something on her plate—the roast beef, Anne believed—and she frowned to herself, wondering whether she should talk to the cook or leave the matter alone.

She was not the only one who noticed Miss Elizabeth's difficulties, however, for Darcy offered up his services to Miss Elizabeth over the young woman's protests.

Miss Elizabeth's cheeks were flushed as she offered her gratitude, and Darcy smiled at her. "It is no trouble at all, Miss Elizabeth. You need only ask should you require assistance." He colored then, as if realizing he had shown too much of his feelings, and he promptly returned his attention to his own plate.

"Your offer is too broad, Mr. Darcy," said Miss Elizabeth. "You should specify only that you wish to provide aid should my cutlery foil me further."

"I do not believe my offer to be too expansive. Rather, whatever aid I can give is gladly yours."

As Anne watched her cousin's dark gaze settle on the young woman, she had to cover her mouth to hide her gasp. She was wrong. Her cousin was not *falling* in love with Miss Elizabeth; rather, he had already fallen completely.

Miss Elizabeth appeared to see something unexpected in his gaze—or perhaps it was the words he offered—as her cheeks darkened even further, and she looked away.

Darcy cleared his throat and began eating once more, and for a few minutes, the pair ate quietly.

Anne began attacking her own plate with a vengeance. She was determined now to find a way to push her cousin closer to Miss Elizabeth by the end of the evening. She needed only to figure out a proper scheme and execute it.

After dinner, while everyone gathered to play the seasonal games she had planned, the first tactic Anne tried was to call her cousin and Miss Elizabeth to stand beneath a sprig of mistletoe under the pretense of showing them a festive piece of décor. The mistletoe had been situated in an out-of-the-way corner of the house, so she did not fear that they would be seen and cause a big to-do. Unfortunately, as Anne attempted to coax an oblivious Elizabeth Bennet to move so that she stood beneath the piece of greenery, Mr. Darcy said: "Miss Bennet, please be wary. There is a piece of mistletoe nearly overhead."

Miss Elizabeth halted her steps and focused on where he was pointing. "Ah, I see what you mean. Thank you, Mr. Darcy. You have saved me from making a most dangerous misstep."

From behind the other young woman, Anne held her hands up in question and tilted her head with a glare, trying to silently demand that her cousin advise as to the reason for overturning her plans.

Darcy merely gave her an innocent look as he responded to Miss Elizabeth. "You are most welcome, Miss Bennet. There are some who would wish to do mischief with such an innocuous-seeming plant."

Anne shook her head in exasperation and then proceeded to complete the rest of her pretense, asking their opinion concerning the placement of an evergreen bough bedecked with ribbons.

Darcy watched her carefully the whole time, and she knew that he, at least, had recognized the thrust of Anne's efforts that evening.

When they joined the rest of the party, a game of Charades soon commenced. Anne attempted to steer the riddles toward themes involving love and courtship, all while spearing Darcy with a meaningful look. These efforts were flatly ignored.

During a game of bullet pudding, she suggested they partner off into pairs of male and female, but everyone except Mrs. Bennet gave her such scandalized expressions that she played off the suggestion as a joke. Perhaps it had not been such a brilliant idea regardless, for the game lent itself more to individuals playing than to teams, but she had started grasping at any opportunity that came to mind.

As the night wore on, Anne began to view her endeavors as hopeless. She would need to rally and ensure she was better prepared the next time she attempted to bring her cousin and Miss Elizabeth closer. Perhaps, she thought, she could involve Georgiana Darcy in the next scheme—once she had concocted one, of course.

There was, however, an unexpected gleam of hope. Over Lady Catherine's protests, it was suggested that a game of Snap-dragon be played.

Anne had not often taken part in Christmas games in the past because of her ill health, but she had long known how the game worked. A wide and low bowl was placed in the center of the table containing heated brandy and a multitude of raisins and almonds. Once the brandy had been set aflame, the lights in the room were extinguished, and everyone watched as the blue flames danced in the shallow bowl over the raisins and almonds.

"I will be the one to snatch the most snap-dragons," proclaimed Lydia Bennet as she removed her gloves, "for you know the one who does shall meet their true love in the coming year!"

"I think you will be disappointed, Lydia," said Kitty Bennet, "for *I* intend to be the one who grabs the most!"

Laughing, the girls started off the game's chant after fully divesting themselves of their gloves, and then they proclaimed themselves to be dragons and demons as they burned their fingers and placed the blazing raisins on their tongues, whereupon they extinguished them by closing their mouths.

Glancing at Darcy and Miss Elizabeth, Anne watched the former lean close to the latter and murmur: "Should you moisten your fingers each time before reaching for a raisin, it shall lessen the incidences of burning."

Miss Elizabeth gave him a look over her shoulder and teased quietly: "That is called cheating, Mr. Darcy!"

"No," said he, "it is merely being protective of your hands. To tell the truth, I have never understood the appeal of this game."

"The appeal is the danger, Mr. Darcy," said Miss Elizabeth with a smile. "Nothing worth having is easy to obtain."

The young woman, who had already removed her gloves, then took her turn at reaching into the bowl. Unfortunately, her two youngest sisters had begun to jostle each other, and Miss Lydia was pushed against her, causing Miss Elizabeth to fall forward, part of her arm splashing into the fiery brandy.

As Miss Elizabeth cried out in pain, Darcy pulled her up out of the bowl and backward. He snapped at the two young Bennets: "You must be more careful!" Then he pulled Miss Elizabeth's bare arm up to examine the afflicted area in the blue light of the flames.

Anne's visibility was limited in part by the dim lighting and by Mrs. Bennet, who had hurried forward to assess the damage, but she thought the young woman's skin bore signs of redness.

"I would suggest you place a cool cloth upon your arm," said Mr. Darcy. "I do not believe there shall be any lasting damage, but your arm faced the lick of the flames for far too long."

"I appreciate your concern, Mr. Darcy, but I shall not perish from a minor burn."

"Lizzy, you must listen to Mr. Darcy," said Mrs. Bennet. "You do not want a blemish to mar your skin. You should allow Mr. Darcy to tend to you and aid you in finding something to soothe the burn."

As Darcy drew the young woman aside, presumably to locate a cloth and moisten it, Anne sighed to herself. Though Darcy had been given the opportunity to show gentle care—and had comported himself nicely—she supposed it was too much to expect the young couple to bond over such a painful experience.

On account of the eagerness of Lydia and Kitty Bennet to resume, the game of Snap-dragon started up once more. Anne, however, withdrew from the game at her mother's worried insistence.

"I have always despised this game," proclaimed Lady Catherine to her daughter, "and I do not believe we should offer it next year."

Anne murmured her own acknowledgment and let her mother continue to rant about her dislike of Snap-dragon and its dangers. As Lady Catherine did so, Anne watched the other revelers laughing and snatching flaming raisins from the bowl, all while pondering what her next move should be. The Christmas party had clearly failed to accomplish her goal. Perhaps she might enlist the aid of Mrs. Bennet next time in addition to Georgiana. She had a feeling Miss Elizabeth's mother would be a willing participant with the proper inducement.

After moistening a towel and wrapping it about Elizabeth's arm, Fitzwilliam pulled her from the room when no one was looking and brought her to the out-of-the-way corner of the house where Anne had taken them earlier in the evening.

"Are you certain you are well?" asked the gentleman quietly, gazing at Elizabeth's covered arm in concern.

"It shall take more than a mishap at Snap-dragon to induce me to tears," said she, favoring him with a smile.

He uncovered her arm and gently caressed the bare red flesh there. "How extreme is the pain you are undergoing?"

"Not extreme at all," said she in reassurance. "There is another subject that I should much rather discuss. Your cousin, Miss de Bourgh, appears to be trying so hard in her matchmaking schemes. Do you think we should at least reveal to her that we are secretly engaged? I fear this latest development may dishearten her."

Fitzwilliam smiled. "I should much prefer not to reward such a busybody. Rather, I think we should make her suffer the agony of not knowing for a little while longer."

Elizabeth laughed. "You are incorrigible."

"I suppose I may be," said he, "but I should like to think that I have also made some improvements to my character since meeting you."

"Indeed, you have."

After glancing around briefly, he pulled her close to him. "I do not know if you noticed, Elizabeth, but you were standing beneath the mistletoe."

"I had noticed," said she. "I was waiting for you to realize it."

Fitzwilliam laughed. "I suppose I cannot disobey the rules of the mistletoe."

"I should be most disappointed if you did."

Fitzwilliam leaned toward Elizabeth, and she closed her eyes in anticipation. Moments later, the butterfly-soft sensation of his lips on hers caused a smile to blossom on her face. But it was not enough, and she pushed forward, deepening the kiss and grabbing at the lapels of his waistcoat to bring him closer to her.

Fitzwilliam chuckled against her mouth in appreciation, and once they had parted, he asked: "Do you believe your father may be available for a call tomorrow? Has his business been properly concluded?"

Elizabeth smiled. "I think he shall be quite at leisure to accept a caller."

"I am glad to hear it. Then perhaps we may soon announce our engagement and relieve my cousin's anxiety."

Mr. Bennet had left for London before Elizabeth had accepted Fitzwilliam's proposal of marriage, so the pair had agreed to maintain the secrecy of their engagement until such time as Mr. Bennet's approval could be secured. It had not always been easy to remain silent on the subject, so the prospect of revealing themselves was quite appealing.

"Perhaps you should encourage Mr. Bingley to accompany you," said Elizabeth casually.

"Should I?"

"Did you not know? Mr. Bingley has proposed marriage to Jane, and she has accepted him."

Fitzwilliam laughed. "I am glad to hear it, but I am surprised he has managed to keep the secret from me."

"It was a recent development, or else you might have heard something. Still, I suspect he is quite proud of having kept the secret from you thus far."

"Yet you are willing to spoil his fun?"

"I do not want to delay my sister's happiness any more than my own. Bring Mr. Bingley with you, and this Christmas season shall become all the happier."

"Consider it settled then. I have no desire for further delay myself. My love for you is too great to maintain such secrecy for long."

Elizabeth gave him a warm look. "Those words are quite pretty, dear sir. Have you further lovers' words to offer?"

"If you desire them, then I shall provide them."

"Perhaps you should compare my eyes to the stars that dot the night sky—or perhaps the snap-dragons whose heated lair so fiercely scorched my arm."

"I should never venture to do so," said Fitzwilliam, "for my anger, once roused, is difficult to quell, and the game of Snap-dragon has drawn my ire most decidedly."

Elizabeth chuckled. "I love you, Fitzwilliam, even if forgiveness shall never come easily to you."

"And I love you, Elizabeth, dearly, deeply, and completely."

The lovers then shared one more kiss under the mistletoe, failing to realize that a bright-eyed Lydia had come upon them, having been sent by her mother to ensure Elizabeth had sustained no lasting injury. Elizabeth and Fitzwilliam's anticipated timeline would soon be shattered, but ultimately, the end result would be the same. Elizabeth and Fitzwilliam would wed, and they would have a happy and fulfilling life together.

Still, neither could ever quite countenance the game of Snap-dragon after that Christmas season, and Fitzwilliam Darcy seemed to bear a particularly strong grudge against it.

The End

THE YULE LOG
Colin Rowland

I came across the tradition of the Yule log and decided it might be nice to explore the possibility of Elizabeth and Mr. Darcy possessing differing opinions on the observance of this tradition.

"*I* do so love the Christmas season," said Elizabeth to Jane as they crossed the expansive snow-covered lawn fronting the Pemberley manor. "Everywhere one travels, the people are happier and their laughter is more easily and often provoked; why, I can even detect a spring in their step. It is not an exaggeration to proclaim this to be my favorite time of the year."

Georgiana had invited Elizabeth and Jane to enjoy the Christmas holiday with her at Pemberley, and the sisters had been quite pleased to accept. The friendship between Mr. Darcy's sister and Elizabeth had grown in the months since Mr. Darcy had begun courting Elizabeth, and Elizabeth now considered Georgiana to be a dear friend.

Elizabeth and Jane had arrived in Derbyshire the previous day in the company of their aunt, Mrs. Gardiner, who had reluctantly agreed to act as chaperone for the visit after Mrs. Bennet begged and cajoled her. Mr. Gardiner and their children had remained at Longbourn for the Christmas celebration, a fact Mrs. Gardiner bemoaned as the trip progressed. Mr. Darcy was himself absent, having accompanied his sister to Lambton to complete her purchases of Christmas gifts.

Mr. Bingley, who had gone to London for the purpose of tending to business affairs, was expected to join the company later in the evening so that he might share in the Christmas observance on the morrow. While walking to the drawing-room earlier that morning and discussing the gentleman's anticipated arrival with Jane, Elizabeth had noticed that none of the staff and servants were bustling about to make the manor ready for Christmas. She had inquired of Mrs. Reynolds and been informed, to her dismay, there were no decorations prepared, as Mr. Darcy did not encourage such. In response, Elizabeth had asked permission of the estate's master to address the lack. Approval had been given, but only grudgingly.

Refusing to be disheartened by Mr. Darcy's unenthusiastic response, Elizabeth had cajoled her sister to accompany her as she explored the estate grounds for growths of holly and ivy with which to decorate the manner. In a wonderful stroke of good fortune, they had even discovered a growth of mistletoe prospering in a stand of evergreens. Elizabeth planned to pluck the sprigs and fashion them into kissing boughs for placement atop a few of the manor doors.

"Is it not time to return?" asked Jane of her sister once morning had become afternoon. "This traipsing around the property and climbing through thickets has given me quite the appetite. May we at least suspend our exploration long enough to assuage our hunger?"

Elizabeth chuckled quietly at the plaintive request. She loved her sister unreservedly but was aware of Jane's antipathy toward spending much time out of doors. Jane much preferred to occupy herself with pastimes she thought more respectable for a young lady. To Jane, a productive day was one spent performing needlework, reading an uplifting book, or composing letters for dispatch to relatives or friends.

In contrast, Elizabeth's fondest memories were of mornings spent walking well-worn paths and exploring the hills and valleys surrounding her home of Longbourn, a habit she intended to continue during her stay at Pemberley.

"Very well," said Elizabeth with a quick laugh. "I certainly would not like my sister to perish from hunger. Before we go, however, let us explore the copse behind the stable. I require some rosemary for the kissing boughs. I spoke yesterday with Mrs. Reynolds, and she informed me some members of the staff have experience in fashioning them, so we can be certain of some aid should we require it.

"Still," continued Elizabeth after a brief pause, "the attitude of the staff seems somewhat odd. When I asked Mr. Darcy's manservant why preparations for the holiday had not yet begun, Mr. Snell said the season has not been commemorated at Pemberley for some time."

"I have heard none of the staff discussing Mr. Darcy's Christmas plans," said Jane, "apart from what Mrs. Reynolds told us this morning."

"It may be Mr. Darcy does not normally spend the holiday at Pemberley but instead with his aunt at Rosings Park. He would not need Christmas finery within the manor should he typically spend the season with Lady Catherine."

"This year may see the establishment of a new tradition," said Jane. "In the future, he will prefer to remain at Pemberley with his wife and children rather than spend it away from his home and treasured friends."

"Has Mr. Darcy acquired a fiancée since last we saw him?" asked Elizabeth with a smile. "If this is so, he has been remiss in advising us. Hurry and gather your possessions so our return to Longbourn is not delayed. I will send for a carriage and locate my aunt, as I have no wish to cause trouble for Mr. Darcy and his soon-to-be wife."

"I refer to you, dear sister, as you well know," said Jane with a laugh. "The man is besotted. He watches your every move and is constantly by your side. When you are together, the rest of the world ceases to exist in his eyes. I am certain you will soon be engaged, possibly even before the week is spent and we return to

Longbourn."

"Where do you find these ideas?" asked Elizabeth, chuckling. "He has given no indication of his undying love for me. I believe your hunger has compromised your intelligence. Let us return posthaste so your intellect may be restored."

Elizabeth set off smartly toward the manor, leaving Jane to catch up as best she could. Upon entrance to the main hall, they shed their outer cloaks and went to locate Mrs. Reynolds in the hope of obtaining a light midday meal.

"Thank you," said Elizabeth when the brunch was completed and the dishes cleared from the table. "Please compliment the cook for her delicious food."

"Thank her for all of us, if you please," said Mrs. Gardiner in agreement with Elizabeth. "I cannot remember a meal I have enjoyed so much."

"I will relay the message," said Mrs. Reynolds as she turned to depart the dining room.

"Might there be small nails available for our use?" asked Elizabeth, her question halting Mrs. Reynolds's progress in crossing the room.

"For what purpose?" asked the housekeeper after a moment of hesitation.

"We need only a small number," said Jane. "The morning's exploration afforded us a sufficient amount of greenery with which to fashion decorations for use in adorning the manor. We will spend the afternoon preparing what we can and intend to place the decorations about the building in time for tomorrow's Christmas celebration."

"Mr. Darcy has not decorated the manor at all since the passing of his father," said Mrs. Reynolds. "In truth, we do not make mention of the season, as it appears to anger him."

"I believe his spirits will be lightened by the festive spirit the decorations will arouse," said Elizabeth with confidence.

"We shall see," said Mrs. Reynolds, her voice carrying a note of doubt as she left the room.

Some minutes passed before she returned. When she did, she held a hammer and a small wooden box containing an assortment of nails. "I have brought what I could find. Please consult with the butler before affixing them to a wall." She gave the box to Elizabeth and departed the room, stopping at the door to regard the two young women as they placed the morning's treasures on the table. Elizabeth, glancing up, took note of the housekeeper's expression of concern mingled with dread, as if the woman were desirous of an outcome different from what she knew was inevitable.

"Will you stay and assist us with the greenery?" asked Elizabeth of Mrs. Gardiner, who shook her head in the negative.

"I thank you for the invitation," said she, "but I am involved in some demanding needlework at present and wish to return to it. Mrs. Reynolds showed me a lovely sewing room with the provisions I will require, and I wish to spend some time there." Nodding to the sisters, the older woman left the room.

The two sisters set to their task and were quickly absorbed in the work of fashioning the wreaths and boughs they considered essential to the proper observance of Christmas.

Elizabeth and Jane toiled without pause until the daylight began to fade and shadows commenced the work of shrouding the room in darkness. At last, when the third and final wreath had been completed, Elizabeth straightened her back, its ache testament to the effort she had expended.

Both sisters surveyed the room, taking note of the wreaths laid upon the table and the pair of kissing boughs waiting to be attached above a doorway.

Jane grasped the signal cord and pulled to summon the housekeeper.

"Please locate Snell," said Elizabeth when Mrs. Reynolds appeared. "The wreaths and boughs are complete, and I need someone to assist with putting them in their places."

"I urge you to reconsider what you are doing," said Mrs. Reynolds. "Mr. Darcy will not appreciate your interference with his established Christmas routine. He has chosen to forego the observance, and we take care to avoid mention of the season in his presence."

"He made no protests before leaving this morning when I informed him of my intentions to display seasonal decorations," said Elizabeth. "His only demand was that they be muted in appearance."

"As you wish," said the woman with a sniff, turning from Elizabeth. "I will ask Mr. Snell to assist you."

"I think you have angered Mrs. Reynolds," said Jane once the woman had left the room. "I hope she does not develop an abiding resentment, for it shall make your position difficult when you are wedded to Mr. Darcy." This last was spoken with a smile which became a laugh as she beheld her sister's mild annoyance.

Before Elizabeth could respond, Mr. Darcy's manservant appeared. "You sent for me, madam?"

"Enough," said Elizabeth to Jane. "If you do not wish to assist me, dear sister, then you may go find your amusement at another's expense while I discuss the decorating of the manor with Mr. Snell."

Jane merely smiled, however, and remained, though she held her tongue.

"Mrs. Reynolds informed me of your intentions to display the decorations of the season," said Mr. Snell to Elizabeth. "I would advise you against such an action, as Mr. Darcy will not receive your efforts kindly."

"Is there no one possessing the joy of Christmas in Pemberley or its environs?" asked Elizabeth, exasperated at the frequent opposition with which she had been beset. "Your master has authorized me to adorn the house with muted decorations, so my sister and I have constructed two kissing boughs as well as some festive wreaths. I have requested your presence because I require your assistance in placing them in appropriate positions. Will you help me accomplish this, or must I complete the task alone?"

"I will participate in your misguided endeavor to instill a sense of Christmas joy in Mr. Darcy," said Mr. Snell, the displeasure in his tone matching his words. "However, I would ask that you consider amending your decision. The master may very well be upset upon discovering such drastic changes have been made to the manor, no matter what he may have expressed in terms of approval."

With Mr. Snell's help, all was made ready for the following day's celebration; the wreaths were attached to the doors, where they would be noticed upon entering the estate, and the kissing boughs were placed above the entryways to the sitting room and the dining room. While the effect was much milder than that which would be found at Longbourn, Elizabeth thought she had abided by Mr. Darcy's request that any alterations made to the house's appearance be minor.

"Thank you for your assistance," said Elizabeth to Mr. Snell when the final decoration had been hung.

"Please, madam, do not mention it," said the man as he walked from the sitting room.

"Ever," he added to himself as he entered the hallway to return to his room. While Elizabeth heard his remark, she chose not to comment upon it.

Having now accomplished their purpose, Elizabeth and Jane took the opportunity to sit and rest. As they did so, Elizabeth pondered the staff's reactions to her attempts at imbuing the manor with some semblance of the joy of the holiday. While she was aware there were some who were not enamored with the season and put little effort into the decorating of their homes and properties, never had she encountered any who opposed its celebration. She was unsettled by the notion that the man whom she had come to love might be against its observance.

"I am sure the staff is mistaken," thought Elizabeth. "Mr. Darcy is a busy man, and in all probability, he has not been afforded the time required to prepare for the festivities."

"They have arrived," said Jane suddenly, interrupting Elizabeth's ruminations.

Looking toward the front hall, Elizabeth saw Mr. Darcy and his sister enter the manor. With haste, she rose from her seat and followed Jane to the entrance hall to welcome the travelers.

Mr. Darcy appeared disturbed as he surveyed the boughs attached to the lintels above the two doors. In Elizabeth's estimation, they were small and plain, bearing none of the refinements of gaily colored paper usually seen at Longbourn. Furthermore, they were simple in their design, each having two sprigs of mistletoe with a branch of berries on either side. The whole was woven together with supple evergreen branches shaped into the form of a spray of greenery. To Elizabeth, their simplicity imbued each with beauty and encouraged one to pluck a berry and offer a kiss under one of them.

"These are the unobtrusive decorations you spoke about this morning?" asked Mr. Darcy. "It seems our definitions of unobtrusive differ. I also do not recall mention of there being anything attached to the surface of my doors, yet they are adorned as well. It was my understanding you wanted to adorn a few of the windows with small trinkets."

"I think they are delightful," said Georgiana in defense of Elizabeth, "and I appreciate the attempts to brighten the dispiriting mood of this hall."

Georgiana had grown since Elizabeth had last seen her some months previous. Her height had increased until she now stood almost at Mr. Darcy's shoulder. The fat of childhood had all but disappeared, leaving a beautiful young woman in its place. Her eyes had assumed some of the intensity of her brother's, so when she gave her attention, it seemed she could peer completely through whoever she was studying. Gone was the shy girl, replaced by a woman confident of her place in the world and the role she would play in guiding her own personal progress.

"You are welcome," said Elizabeth in reply. "I am pleased you find my efforts adequate, as I was unsure of the level of talent I possessed when beginning to craft the wreaths."

"Well, I find them to be wonderful," said Georgiana. She then looked at her brother. "Do you not agree?"

"It is much too ostentatious," said he in disgruntled tones as he turned to direct the placement of Georgiana's trunk, which had been unloaded from the coach.

"Never you mind," said Georgiana. "I like it, and you could as well if you would only forget the past and acknowledge the present."

"I cannot forget, and neither should you!" said Mr. Darcy, his voice rising. He then turned on his heel and left the room, anger evident in the set of his shoulders.

"Have I caused offense?" wondered Elizabeth aloud. "If so, it was unintended."

"Do not be troubled," said Georgiana. "The Christmas season is one of sorrow for my brother, and Christmas Eve is especially so. It was on this day five years ago that our father passed from this earth. My brother has not celebrated the day since then and forbids the servants to make mention of it to him, although he does not begrudge them their own observance of the holiday."

"Had I known," said Elizabeth, "I should never have raised the subject. I will remove them at once."

"Wait," said Georgiana, placing her hand on Elizabeth's arm to delay her. "He gave his approval when you raised the subject; he cannot rescind it now. My brother and I will speak privately later, as we have each Christmas since our father's passing, and I will discuss the issue with him then. I do not believe he feels antipathy toward the season itself; he simply cannot bring himself to regain the joy he once possessed."

"I should be the one to speak with him," said Elizabeth, "so that I might apologize for my insensitive actions."

"It will be better to leave him be until he joins us this evening. At that time, his anger should have run its course, and he will hopefully have realized the foolishness of his behavior.

"Now, show me what you have done to brighten Pemberley manor in preparation for Christmas Day."

Elizabeth took Georgiana to see the wreaths and boughs she had created with Jane. Georgiana, ever the polite young woman, praised the Bennet sisters' ingenuity in crafting the ornaments from the scant supplies they had located.

Elizabeth felt an intimacy with Mr. Darcy's sister that she had never experienced before, even with Charlotte Lucas. In Georgiana, Elizabeth saw a young woman growing into her responsibilities as the daughter of a prominent house. In the months since Elizabeth had last seen her, the girl had matured in stature and in demeanor, as had been witnessed with the self-assurance she had shown in standing her ground against Mr. Darcy's outburst.

When at last Georgiana had been shown all of the decorations that had been crafted, she and the two Bennet sisters took seats in the sitting room to share the important news of the time.

"Georgiana," said Elizabeth when the conversation had run its course, "are you privy to the location of the unburnt piece of the previous Yule log?" Tradition demanded that the new one be lit with an unburnt portion of the one from the previous year, but Elizabeth had hesitated to broach the subject due to the staff's reactions to any discussion of Christmas traditions.

Georgiana looked with wide eyes at the hearth, upon which rested a timber too immense to be safely burned. In apparent awe, she leaned toward Elizabeth. "I noted the wood at the hearth when we entered the room but did not realize you had made plans to observe this tradition. Is it important to you that we do so? It has been so long since the Yule log was lit in the manor house that there may not be a fragment remaining to be found."

The two Bennet sisters and Georgiana turned as they heard Mr. Darcy enter the room. He opened his mouth, as if to say something, only to close it as he glanced at the hearth. After observing it for a moment, his face showed his realization that the freshly cut timber held a special significance.

His voice holding an undercurrent of hostility, he asked: "Might I ask why such a large log has been set in the fireplace?"

"I asked the groundsman to cut it and place it on the grate," said Elizabeth steadily. She recognized Mr. Darcy's growing anger, but the tradition of the Yule log was one with which she never intended to be parted. "It is to serve as the Yule log, which will imbue the manor with good fortune throughout the coming year. It needs only a fragment from the last one to light it."

"This has gone beyond the bounds of what I can endure," said Mr. Darcy in a tone which brooked no dissent. "I granted your request to decorate Pemberley, provided your decorations were small and unassuming, but my wishes were not heeded. I said nothing to Georgiana when she belittled my opinion and adopted your own, but my efforts seem to remain unappreciated. I have attempted to maintain serenity amidst the uproar you have brought to Pemberley despite my inclination to do otherwise. I was willing, and somewhat eager, to pay no mind to the disregard for my wishes, which is a testament to the depth of my attachment for you.

"I cannot, however, tolerate this assault upon what for me was once the very essence of Christmas. This was the evening I relished most of the season. It was on this night our Yule log was lit; it was a time for reflection and discussion concerning the twelvemonth past. The year my father honored me with the solemn duty of lighting the log is one I will cherish forever. I cannot allow your actions to dilute the memory of joyful Christmases past.

"Snell!" said he, his call bringing the servant at a rapid gait into the room. "Have one of the stable hands assist you in removing this log from the house."

"Where should I take it?" asked Mr. Snell.

"It matters not," said Mr. Darcy. "As long as it is not to be found in the manor, it can be disposed of anywhere you find convenient. Give it to one of the tenants or add it to the wood pile."

"Please do not remove it from the house," pleaded Elizabeth as Mr. Snell went in search of assistance. "The tradition of the Yule log has been observed in the Bennet family for generations and is among my most cherished of memories. All in my house eagerly anticipate its lighting each Christmas Eve.

"I beg of you, Mr. Darcy—please allow the presence of this burning timber to establish newer, joyous recollections, ones which you will have cause to call upon with fond remembrance for years to come."

"I have no need to replace the memories of my father," said Mr. Darcy firmly. "They are all I have left of him; I will not allow them to fade until he is no more thought of than last evening's meal. I cherish the recollections I possess and will not have them relegated to the distant past."

"I suggest nothing of the sort," replied Elizabeth. "I encourage you to remember your dear father with every fiber of your being, clinging to your memories and holding them close to your heart. I take no issue with your doing so. Rather, Mr. Darcy, I would encourage you to realize that your refusal to permit new experiences will only cause further anguish as time inevitably dims those recollections of your father. If you do not open your heart to the creation of additional images of tender moments, you will erect a wall of armor about your heart which can do naught but leave you lonely and unhappy, having only distant recollections dimmed with age until they are no more."

Mr. Darcy's head shook from one side to another as Elizabeth pleaded with him. Looking up, she peered into his eyes, wanting to find some glimmer of understanding and compromise, but in this, she was to be disappointed.

"Snell!" shouted he. "What is delaying you? Remove this timber from the manor at once.

"I cannot permit your removal of every memory I hold dear," said he to Elizabeth.

Unfortunately, Elizabeth's anger at his intractability had reached its limit. "If this is your final decision, then so be it. Your memory of Christmas with your father has become a shrine to him in your thoughts. I cannot remain in a home that is no more than a mausoleum, where joy and friendship are cast aside in fear of disturbing recollections of occurrences long since passed. If you could be so kind as to direct Mrs. Gardiner's coach to be readied, we will return to Longbourn to celebrate Christmas in a kinder, more joyous location."

Her decision rendered, Elizabeth turned and fled from the room.

"It was a mistake of monumental proportions to extend the invitation in the first place," growled Mr. Darcy to himself. "It is not one I shall ever be tempted to make again." Irate, he left the room for another shortly down the hall, his entry into the room accompanied by a slamming of the door that possessed such force it shook the surrounding walls.

"What shall we do?" asked Georgiana once she and Jane had found Mrs. Gardiner and explained what had happened. "I fear this argument has opened a chasm too difficult to cross, for the pride of each has been wounded and might never be assuaged."

"I will speak with Elizabeth," said Mrs. Gardiner. "She is a reasonable girl, although headstrong. She and I have always been close; I have no doubt she will listen. Whether she can be persuaded against departing, however, is something I cannot predict."

"I thank you," said Georgiana. "In the meantime, I will undertake to speak with my brother."

Leaving the sitting room, Georgiana approached the door behind which her brother had hidden. After taking a deep breath to prepare herself, she knocked with a firm hand.

"Enter," came the short answer, upon which she turned the knob and let herself into the room. Fitzwilliam was seated at his desk, the windows behind him displaying a dreary day, the mood of which had seemingly penetrated the manor itself.

Georgiana seated herself on the settee and regarded her brother. Even now, when he was at his most stubborn, she was fond of him.

Still, his actions today were cause for concern. She had known of the special bond between father and son and had always looked up to her brother in pride because of it. What had, until today, escaped her notice was the depth of despair he felt in the loss of their father some years before. In truth, Mrs. Reynolds had on occasion alluded to changes in Fitzwilliam since that Christmas Eve, but in the insensitivity born of youth, Georgiana had dismissed them as unimportant.

The argument Georgiana had witnessed had shocked and frightened her. The brother she observed in disagreement with Miss Elizabeth was unrecognizable, someone she had no wish of seeing again.

Georgiana gathered her resolve and began: "Your mood troubles me, Brother. Miss Elizabeth meant no disrespect in placing the block upon the hearth; her desire was to lighten your mood and inspire you to partake of the joy of the Christmas celebration."

Her brother glowered at her, his anger at the perceived insult reminding her of a white-hot canker that burned within and would, she surmised, never recede unless she could reach the kind-hearted man who still dwelt inside.

"She has overstepped her bounds," said he, "and refuses to acknowledge her offense."

"She was not attempting to show disservice to the memories of our father," said Georgiana. "Her only crime was her attempt to instill the wonder of this most joyous of seasons in the hearts of all who reside within the bounds of Pemberley. Her observation of the mausoleum-like quality found within these walls is far too accurate for comfort, and I feel certain you will agree if you can find it within yourself to pay honest attention to the issue."

"She knows not of what she speaks," insisted Mr. Darcy. "I choose to forego decorations commemorating a celebration in which I find no joy; I do not prohibit the servants and tenants their observance, nor would I attempt to do so."

"If this is true, then why did you make a decision so foolhardy as to invite Elizabeth and Miss Bennet to partake of the season with you? You, of all people, should have suspected that the lively Elizabeth would have a penchant for celebrating Christmas with an overabundance of zeal. Did you assume her love of the holiday would temper itself until her return to Longbourn?

"I fear you have turned her away in a most fearsome and inhospitable manner, and in so doing, you have forfeited her love. I adjure you, Brother: go to her and beg for her forgiveness. If you do not, you will find yourself alone and miserable, with no one to share your joys or your sorrows."

Georgiana rose and, after one final sight of her brother, left the room. In her heart burned a desire to see the two, her closest friend and her dear brother, mend their differences and come together in love once again, but ensnarled in her thoughts was the fear that an irreversible decision had been made.

Mrs. Gardiner sat in Elizabeth's room, watching the girl as she emptied drawers and closets, throwing clothing and jewelry into her trunks in an untidy heap.

"He had no right to treat me in that way," said Elizabeth to her aunt, whipping a pair of gloves up in the air as if she wished to strike Mr. Darcy with them. "I meant no harm in my attempts to bring cheer to this depressing estate."

"While your intentions were good, I believe it was your actions with which Mr. Darcy took exception," said Mrs. Gardiner. "My understanding is that he was incensed by the notion you wished to erase the imprint of his father upon his character. I know you, Lizzy, and I can see you have been hurt by what you perceive as his callous disregard for your wish to infuse the manor with the spirit of Christmas. Please do not fall into the trap of perceiving insult where none was intended."

"He is an insufferable brute," said Elizabeth, anger still smoldering within her. "That he should presume my intentions were such as he described was the vilest of insults. I will not allow him the pleasure of mistreating me further."

"I do not believe Mr. Darcy derived any pleasure from his assessment of your motives or your disposition toward the memory of his father. Rather, I believe he venerates the man and will fight to his last breath to preserve the image of him in his mind. His lashing out at you was nothing more than a response to his fear of losing something he holds dear. In this, you should not judge him too harshly."

Elizabeth sat in a chair by the window, having paused at her aunt's counsel. Her anger, while still aroused by the words she had exchanged with Mr. Darcy, was abating as she took time to consider the points her aunt had raised. Sympathy for Mr. Darcy attempted to arise within but was quickly tamped down as she fought to defend her feelings of rejection and misuse. Unwilling to retract her wounded pride, she resumed packing until in exasperation she noted she was alone in her activity.

"Have you already made ready to depart?" inquired she of her aunt. "Shall I be the last to complete my preparations?"

"Let us wait, Elizabeth," said Mrs. Gardiner in a voice so soft Elizabeth strained to interpret the words. "Tomorrow is Christmas. It is not a day for travel, but rather for quiet observance with family and friends. Longbourn will be there if we wait a day or two, and travel in this season is so much improved when undertaken with proper preparation. We may delay our departure until then with no harm aroused."

Elizabeth looked to her aunt, wondering at the hesitation she heard in the words. Were there unknown motives in her suggestion, or was there wisdom in her desire to postpone their leaving Pemberley? In confusion, Elizabeth again paused and sat beside her aunt, hoping for comfort and reassurance.

"If you are certain it would be better to delay our departure," said Elizabeth, "then I will abide by your decision." Slowly, she put her head on Mrs. Gardiner's shoulder and closed her eyes, intending to rest them for just a moment. In minutes, however, she was asleep, the tension of the day having worn her down.

Her aunt gently placed the sleeping girl upon the bed and covered her with a blanket before removing herself from the room. She closed the door behind her and went in search of Georgiana. She at last found her in the sitting room, where she was involved in earnest discussion with Jane.

"Elizabeth is asleep," said Mrs. Gardiner. "The disagreement with Mr. Darcy has upset her greatly, but I was able to calm her, and she has agreed to spend the night at Pemberley and delay our departure for Longbourn by a few days. Did you have better success with Mr. Darcy, or was the attempt frivolous?"

"My brother is a loving and kind man until he feels he has been mistreated," said Georgiana. "Our conversation was not as fruitful as

I had hoped, for he is as obstinate as he is charitable. I urged him to make amends and repair the damage, but I fear it is too late."

When Elizabeth awoke on Christmas morning, she was by herself, Mrs. Gardiner having left her the previous evening. Throwing off her covers, she dressed quickly and approached the door, intent on partaking of a hearty breakfast to lift her. As she opened the bedroom door, however, her thoughts returned to the prior evening and her argument with Mr. Darcy.

Her review of the words thrown in the heat of the moment brought shame and sorrow. After experiencing the distance provided by a night's sleep, she now recognized Mr. Darcy's desperate attempt to maintain treasured memories of his father. Her failure to acknowledge his continued love for the man who had been lost to him was an affliction on her sense of self-worth. She wondered how she could have ever been so callous.

As she descended the stairs, her attention was captured by the sound of lowered voices coming from the sitting room. Curious, she approached the entrance and gasped as she saw the very log over which she had fought Mr. Darcy burning merrily in the fireplace. Before it stood Mr. Darcy and Georgiana, locked in a discussion too soft for her to understand. With them was Mr. Bingley, who must have arrived while they slept. He turned upon noting Elizabeth's entrance, and she could sense the slight disappointment in his demeanor as he realized she was not Jane.

When Georgiana saw Elizabeth, she touched Mr. Darcy's hand and nodded toward the doorway Elizabeth occupied. In a whisper, Georgiana made a final remark to her brother before gesturing for Mr. Bingley to follow her and approaching Elizabeth with a smile upon her face.

"Hear him," said Georgiana in passing as she and Mr. Bingley exited the room, leaving Elizabeth and Mr. Darcy as its only occupants.

"I see the timber burning on the hearth," said Elizabeth, unsure of herself and the reaction she would engender in Mr. Darcy. "Forgive my temerity, but it is a beautiful reminder of the reason for the celebration of this holiday."

At the obvious confusion upon his face, she continued her explanation: "To me, the Yule log has always represented the best of Christmas. The timber burning suggests a cleansing of the trials and tribulations of the year past, while the tradition of setting it alight with a remnant of the previous log speaks of new birth, such as was the case on the first Christmas Day so many years ago. I cannot help but contemplate the birth of the baby in the manger and the hope it gives to us all.

"It is my fervent desire that you can find it in your heart to forgive my foolish behavior. I became so involved in my desire to transform Pemberley into a copy of our observances at Longbourn that I neglected to account for the distress I inadvertently caused you and Georgiana. Please do not let my sins further taint this most perfect of days."

Mr. Darcy's heart softened as he heard Elizabeth's heartfelt plea and witnessed the tears traveling down her cheeks. In shame, he bowed his head, unable to find the courage to gaze into the beautiful eyes of this woman whom he loved most in the world.

"It is I who must beg your forgiveness," said he. "I have held to the past far too long. In doing so, I faced the danger of discounting the love I feel growing within my heart. If not for Georgiana's persistence and unwillingness to accept my prideful and haughty airs, I might have been deprived of your smiling wit and cheerful composure forever. I have acted abominably and find it necessary to throw myself at your feet in the hope that you can overlook my inadequacies and remain at Pemberley for the entirety of the Christmas season, as you had first planned."

"But what of your memories of the previous Christmas seasons? Are you not concerned they will be swept away by changes you will be forced to accept?"

"As was pointed out, by both you and my sister, those recollections will forever be part of the commemoration of this day. They will not be supplanted but, rather, enhanced by those we will create together in the years to come."

"Mr. Darcy," said Elizabeth shyly, "are you asking for my hand in marriage?"

"I dare not make such an undertaking," said he with a smile and a quick wink, "until I am in closer proximity to your father, that I might immediately seek permission after you have agreed to accept my offer.

"Furthermore," added he in a whisper only Elizabeth could hear, "should I ask and receive your acceptance, I would no longer be able to enjoy your company over the remainder of this joyous season, as proper decorum would insist you leave the estate. As a result, I think such a question is best saved for another time."

The joy which appeared upon Elizabeth's visage lasted until her departure for Longbourn—and indeed until long after she was again at her home in Hertfordshire.

The End

NO GREATER LOVE

Jann Rowland

I do not often write of Darcy and Elizabeth after they are married, as I usually prefer imagining them coming together in various ways. As I was contemplating different traditions, the ones associated with St. Stephen's Day, also called Boxing Day, made me wonder what Elizabeth's first Christmas might be like if she was determined to fill the role of mistress that had been vacant for so long.

"**S**hall I search for her?"

The question hung in the air, those present in the room gazing at the new mistress as if she were spouting nonsense. But Elizabeth was perfectly serious in her offer. Upon arriving, the tenants had gathered their children together to meet with the new mistress of the estate, but while the three children were standing in a dutiful line before her, her keen hearing had heard and understood the muted comments concerning a fourth child, a girl called Jenny who could be found nowhere.

"Mistress," ventured the footman, a young man by the name of Jack, "I think that would be unwise."

"We can find Jenny ourselves, Mrs. Darcy," added Mrs. Johnson, the tenant's wife. "There be no call for you to search for our wayward child."

"On the contrary," said Elizabeth, pointing back out the front door, "it will take all of us to ensure your daughter's safety, for the weather is worsening as we speak."

It was nothing less than the truth, for the soft flakes which had fallen about the estate, coating all in a soft, white blanket, had become heavier, whipped about by a sudden increase in the wind. William, the sweet man that he was, had worried for Elizabeth's safety when she had departed that morning, predicting the arrival of a winter storm by the evening.

"Oh, I suppose you can predict the winter, having lived here all your life?" Elizabeth had said to him noting his widening smile at her saucy impertinence. He had always claimed he appreciated the liveliness of her mind and the confidence she displayed.

"I think that is not possible for anyone," had been William's reply. "But yes, my residence at Pemberley has given me a certain insight into the weather. I expect we shall experience a bad storm before evening falls."

"I understand and will hurry through the deliveries," said Elizabeth, not wanting to worry him, "but I am determined to proceed as planned, William. Though Georgiana has performed admirably, Pemberley has not had a true mistress since your mother's passing. At Longbourn, it is a tradition for the mistress to distribute boxes for St. Stephen's Day, and it is a tradition I mean to institute here as well."

It seemed William had seen enough of her determination to know when she would not yield, for he did not protest further. "Very well. But I shall send a footman to assist with the deliveries and ensure you return home in safety."

"Oh, do you not think your driver is capable of the feat?"

"Mr. Walsh's skills are not in question. But it would be of comfort to me if Jack also accompanied you."

"Then I accept," said Elizabeth. "His assistance will be welcome, I am sure." After a quick kiss, Elizabeth had ordered the sledge loaded so she could make her deliveries. Though there was a smaller carriage available for journeys about the property, Elizabeth had been grateful there was just enough snow to allow her to go by sledge, for there was rarely enough snow in Hertfordshire for such a treat. Now, however, the snow was a hindrance, and the pending winter storm a danger, for little Jenny needed to be found quickly.

"Do you know where she might have gone?" asked Elizabeth, determined to be of use to these people.

The husband and wife exchanged a look before Mrs. Johnson ventured: "She likes to play down by the brook, though the nearby strand of trees is also a favorite of hers."

"Then I shall go toward the brook," said Elizabeth, "while everyone else can look in a different location. If we depart now, we should return home with your daughter soon."

"Thank you, Mrs. Darcy," said an obviously relieved Mrs. Johnson. "I am sure I will speak to Jenny for causing this trouble."

"Not at all," replied Elizabeth with a warm smile. "Should you have occasion to hear my mother speak of me when I was a girl, I am certain you would hear similar tales of my exploits."

Elizabeth soon had the searchers organized. Besides her and Jack, the driver and the girl's father had been pressed into service. Mr. Walsh, just as Jack had, looked on Elizabeth as if she were daft, but unlike the footman, he said nothing, content instead to mutter under his breath. With a final few words of exhortation, Elizabeth commenced the search.

It quickly became apparent that Elizabeth had miscalculated the imminent nature of the approaching storm, not to mention the ferocity it was to attain. The wind blew harder every moment, and the snowflakes were becoming finer, turning to little pellets that stung the skin of her face as she pressed on. Though the land had already been covered by heavy snowflakes lazily drifting down from a heavy, grey sky, now the finer variety was just as swiftly building the drifts higher due to the simple fact of how hard it was now snowing, to say nothing of the wind whipping them about in some frenetic dance.

Though Elizabeth had always felt herself to be a hardy soul, she soon began to worry for her safety. Still, she continued to search and call out, motivated by the thought of a girl of only five years wandering in this weather at the mercy of the driving snow.

It was a trick of the wind, the imaginings of a fertile mind, but as she pressed on, Elizabeth thought she heard the sound of voices. The cold, which was becoming bitterer by the moment, told her she was risking life and limb for a girl she had never met. The wind shrieked in her ear, telling her it was pointless, that she would never locate the young girl before she collapsed because of the cold and exhaustion. Mustering a grim determination, Elizabeth pushed the voices screaming at her aside and pushed herself forward. Though she could not say how long she had been fighting against the storm, at last an answer to her calls came.

"Help!" cried a small voice.

At first, Elizabeth thought she might have imagined it, but then it sounded again: "Help!"

"Jenny!" called Elizabeth, trying to gain her bearings in the white landscape.

"Here!" came the response.

Following the direction in which she thought the voice had originated, Elizabeth found a small clump of trees. Huddled at the base of one tall oak squatted a pretty young girl sniffling in distress. Elizabeth crouched down and gathered the little girl in close, sheltering her from as much of the wind as she could.

"Jenny, you have given us all a fright!"

"I just wanted to play," said the whimpering little girl. "I meant no trouble."

"Yes, my dear, I know. But now we must see to returning you home."

Doing as she suggested, however, was not as easy as saying it. The whiteness of the landscape offered no discerning features by which she could navigate, and as the wind howled ever louder in their ears, she knew it would be difficult to find the house again. Walking past it out into the middle of Pemberley's fields, confused by the ferocity of the storm might even prove fatal.

"Shelter," murmured Elizabeth to herself as she pulled her pelisse tighter around her frame. "We must find shelter."

Jenny said nothing, her continued whimpering sounding strangely comforting in Elizabeth's ears. Knowing at once that to stay there was death, Elizabeth rose and looked back the way she had come. Though she knew the direction they must go, she might as well have been facing a wall, for the white barrier of winter flakes appeared solid to her tired eyes in the fading light. Left with no other choice, Elizabeth gathered the girl to her and steeled herself for the coming fight, only to pause as a thought occurred to her.

"There is a shack by the brook near the small waterfall!" said Elizabeth to herself.

At Elizabeth's words, the young girl stopped whimpering and looked up into her face. "Yes, I have played there!"

"Now, we need only determine which direction to take," said Elizabeth, feeling uneasy, knowing it would be difficult to find in all this snow. The brook was not far distant, perhaps only a few hundred yards in the opposite direction from which she had come. The small hut she had seen once or twice while walking would provide at least a hint of shelter and perhaps even a means for creating a fire if they could reach it, but should they choose the wrong direction in their attempt to reach the hut, they might walk until exhaustion set in.

"I can find it, Miss," said Jenny.

Elizabeth looked down at the cherubic face staring up at her, surprised at the transformation that had taken place. In contrast with the misery that had cloaked her when the pair had first met, Jenny was now filled with determination and purpose.

"You know where it is?" asked Elizabeth.

"If we walk to the brook and go that way," said the girl, pointing to her right, "it is not far."

"Then let us be off," said Elizabeth, grasping the child's hand in hers.

It was a difficult journey, though Elizabeth thought it did not take them much more than five or ten minutes to accomplish. The wind howled when the pair left the dubious protection of the trees, and for a moment, Elizabeth thought they might become disoriented in the storm. But they fought on, endeavoring to veer neither right nor left, and they soon came to the banks of the now-frozen brook.

Having reached their first objective, Elizabeth glanced down at Jenny and pointed to the right, raising her eyebrow in question. When Jenny nodded without hesitation, Elizabeth decided to trust her, and she turned them in the direction the girl had indicated. The walking here was even more difficult, as the banks of the small river brought small rises which were quickly collecting great drifts of snow.

At length, when the dark outline of the hut rose before them only a short distance from the brook, Elizabeth could have cried with relief. The door was set in the south side of the building, away from the river, and swung open easily when Elizabeth pushed on the handle. Inside, a small room was revealed to their eager eyes, devoid of furnishings except for a rickety chair in one corner and a rough bed in another. There were, she noted, a small, yet inadequate, pile of wood near the door, several old blankets folded and stacked on the bed, and several furs piled near the hearth. A sigh of relief escaped Elizabeth's lips; at least with those blankets, they would not freeze overnight.

"I will search for some firewood," said Elizabeth, crouching down next to Jenny. "It will make our stay more pleasant if we can start a fire."

"The pile is around the back," said the girl. "I saw it when I was playing."

"Then let me gather it," said Elizabeth, rising again to her feet.

Admonishing the girl to stay within, Elizabeth braved the storm once again, moving to the back of the building to find the wood Jenny had seen. Though it was blanketed in snow, Elizabeth knocked it clear of whatever covering she could before taking it into the house and stacking it beside the door. Soon Elizabeth had a pile of wood which would more than carry them through the night if they managed to start a fire.

"Look what I found!" cried Jenny as Elizabeth closed and latched the door again.

Indeed, the young girl had found a treasure. Under the pile of furs which Jenny had moved away from the fireplace was a small hamper containing meticulously stacked rows of kindling and a pile of smaller twigs, branches, and reeds that could be used to start a fire. Furthermore, on the mantle above them sat an old tinderbox which contained the flint and tinder they needed.

"It seems someone has kept this hut stocked and ready for use," commented Elizabeth, thinking she knew who would care for such seemingly minor concerns.

"Can you build a fire with these, Miss?" asked Jenny.

"I can," said Elizabeth. "My father taught me how to do so many years ago when I was only a little older than you to assist me in just such a situation as this."

The girl attended her, curiosity written upon her cherubic face as Elizabeth pulled the necessary items from the basket and took several logs from the pile by the door. As her father had taught her, she arranged the items, putting the smallest at the bottom and the kindling above. Over it all, she leaned two larger pieces of wood from the dry pile inside the hut rather than the wetter pieces she had brought in from the outside. Then she struck the flint, creating sparks and causing

Jenny to gasp. Soon, the sparks ignited the smaller pieces and the flames started to lick their way up the kindling. Within ten minutes, there was a small yet cheery blaze burning, already warming the room from its frigid state.

"You know a lot, Miss," said Jenny, gazing wide-eyed at Elizabeth. "Who are you? I have not seen you before."

"Oh, I have not lived here for long," said Elizabeth, not wishing to frighten the girl by informing her of her status as the master's wife. "But I am sure we shall be well acquainted by the time we are able to leave tomorrow."

Jenny, seeming to sense that Elizabeth was holding back, looked at her for a few moments. Then she appeared to decide it did not matter and turned her attention back to the fire, putting her hands out to warm them against the chill.

"Come," said Elizabeth after a moment. "We should remove our sodden coats and dry them, or we will remain cold."

"Shall we not be colder if we remove our coats?" asked Jenny. "And our dresses are wet also."

"The room is warm enough now," said Elizabeth, unbuttoning her pelisse. "When it becomes a little warmer, we shall also remove our dresses so they can dry."

Soon, they were situated on the furs with blankets—which they had discovered were only a little dusty—around them. Elizabeth had hung their dresses and coats over the chair which she had moved close to the fire. They felt cozy before long, and the extra fuel Elizabeth had added to the fire had urged the flames higher, such that the room was now almost comfortable. As Elizabeth sat before the fire, gazing into its depths with a drowsy little girl propped up against her, she thought of her wonderful husband. He must be almost frantic with worry for her. She would make it up to him, she decided, when the opportunity presented itself. Though the weather made it impossible, she knew he would dispatch searchers the following morning as soon as it was light out, and they would be discovered quickly. For the present, there was nothing for them to eat and they were both hungry, and Elizabeth was grateful Jenny did not complain, seeming to recognize there was nothing they could do except wait until morning.

"Do you know any Christmas stories?" asked Jenny after some time of sitting together in this fashion.

"I know some," said Elizabeth. "I can tell them to you if you like, though I do not know how interesting they will be. Did you enjoy Christmas with your family?"

"Oh, yes," said Jenny, her youthful enthusiasm shining in her countenance. "I received a new dolly."

"I hope you did not lose your dolly in the storm," said Elizabeth with a smile.

"No, she is at home, silly," replied Jenny with a giggle. "She knows better than to play in the snow."

"I hope you have learned a similar lesson," said Elizabeth.

"Yes, Miss," was the girl's solemn reply. "My Mama often tells me not to run off to play, but sometimes I forget. I shall not do so again."

"That is all your Mama can ask."

"Do you think she will be very angry with me?"

Elizabeth put an arm around the little girl. "I should think your Mama will be so happy to see you that she will not be angry for long."

"I hope not," said Jenny, burrowing up next to her. "I do not like it when my Mama is angry."

"That is a sentiment I can well understand," said Elizabeth, remembering how often she had vexed her own mother as a child.

"Story?" reminded Jenny.

Willing to oblige and eager to pass the time in this way, Elizabeth began to relate some of the stories she had heard as a girl. Though Jenny did not comment often, Elizabeth could see that she listened intently, occasionally releasing a sigh or an exclamation of surprise at certain points. Elizabeth's stories consisted of the account of the birth of the Savior and the visit of the wise men, interspersed with more amusing tales she and Jane had often told each other and a ghost story or two. After some time of this, Jenny appeared content, resting against her, her eyes drooping closed in drowsiness.

Elizabeth had found herself drifting off to slumber when she heard the rattling of the latch on the door. Looking up in surprise and a little trepidation as she clutched a blanket to herself to protect her modesty, she began to rise. Suddenly, a man appeared in the doorway wearing a greatcoat and beaver hat, with snow heaped on his shoulders. It was the well-loved face she had come to know intimately these past few months.

"William?" whispered Elizabeth, Jenny starting by her side.

The gentleman looked at her once with unmistakable relief and then retreated back out into the darkness. The sound of two shots rang out, echoing from one end of the broad valley to the other. Then he entered once again and closed the door behind him before turning to look at the two standing together before the fire, huddled in blankets.

"I am happy you have been found, Jenny. Your mother is almost frantic with worry."

"Mr. Darcy!" squeaked the girl, dropping into a hasty approximation of a curtsey.

"Why are you here, William?" cried Elizabeth, hurrying forward to assist her husband.

She helped him divest his greatcoat, hanging it on the chair in place of her and Jenny's coats. Elizabeth fussed about her husband, noting with relief that his coat had protected his jacket from becoming wet, all the while muttering about his foolishness in braving the storm.

"Was I any more foolish than you, Mrs. Darcy?" asked the man, gazing upon her with a stern fondness.

Jenny squeaked yet again. "You are Mrs. Darcy?"

"I am," said Elizabeth, throwing a hard look at her husband. "But do not let that bother you, Jenny, for I am still the same lady with whom you have shared this hut today."

The girl managed a smile and sat back down on her fur, leaving Elizabeth to turn back to her husband. With a glare, Elizabeth said: "I will have you know, Mr. Darcy, that I am an excellent walker and well able to care for myself."

"And I shall have *you* know, Mrs. Darcy," said her husband, "that I have lived here all my life and could walk from one end of Pemberley to the other blindfolded." William paused and gazed at her with his heart in his eyes before leaning down to place a chaste kiss on her lips. "I am grateful I found you, my dear, though I will confess I suspected I would find you here when I heard of the direction you took in your search. I knew I would not sleep tonight if I remained in the house and waited until the morning. And now that I have found you, the rest of the estate may rest easy too."

"Those gunshots?" asked Elizabeth.

"One for each of you," confirmed William, fixing Jenny with a cross-eyed grin which caused the girl to giggle. "Had I only found one of you, I would only have shot once, though no one on the estate would have slept for fear for you both."

Elizabeth sighed. "That is well, then. I knew you would all worry throughout the night, but I had no way to inform you of our safety."

"And safety it certainly is," said William. He led her to the furs and sat down by her side next to Jenny; then he gestured to the fire. "It seems to me you are a woman of many hidden talents, Elizabeth. I did not know you knew how to start a fire."

"Papa taught me when I was a girl," replied Elizabeth. "Though I have rarely had cause to put my skills to use, I am a quick learner and retain what I learn."

"That much is clear, my dear. And for that, I cannot be more grateful."

William ensured the fire was well-tended throughout that entire night, going outside on one occasion to gather more wood and ensure their store would last until morning. It was not long before Jenny, exhausted from the exertions of the day, fell asleep next to the hearth, and while William thought to leave her there, Elizabeth insisted on placing her in the bed with blankets to cover her. A short time later, Elizabeth was nestled next to her husband on a bed of furs, comfortable in front of the fire.

"How did you know we would be here?" asked Elizabeth after some time of staring at the fire in silence.

She felt her husband's shrug. "I know you have walked in this area in the short time since we arrived, and I knew you were searching in this direction. None of the other searchers found Jenny, and it seemed likely that you had come across her and that you had sought shelter. This is the only suitable place nearby."

Concerned, Elizabeth raised herself up on an elbow, gazing into her husband's well-loved face. "What would you have done if you had not found me here? Would you have used the hut for shelter and waited out the storm?"

The hesitation before his response told Elizabeth all she needed to know. "If I had not had confirmation of your safe return, then there is every chance I might have continued to search," said he, seeming to understand there was no reason to dissemble.

With a sigh, Elizabeth laid her head back down on his shoulder. "Then I suppose we should be grateful I *was* here and consider the matter no more."

"That would be my preference," replied William. "I am not one for agonizing about what might have been." He paused and gave a rumbling laugh. "Actually, I suppose these past months have given the lie to that statement, seeing how much I have reflected on how I went wrong in wooing a certain young lady of my acquaintance."

Elizabeth could not help but join him in laughter, though hers was tempered with guilt for her own thoughts and actions. As William had previously informed her of much of his struggles in the months between his proposal and their meeting at Pemberley, there was no reason to ask for clarification. The matter was one she did not wish to consider at any length anyway. It was in the past. There was much in the present of which she could think at length.

"I believe this adventure of yours will do much for your reputation, my dear," said William after a short silence between them.

"The tenants will all think their mistress is fit for Bedlam, will they?" asked Elizabeth.

Again, the sound of his laughter heartened her. "On the contrary, when they understand you were willing to risk life and limb for a little girl you had never met, I suspect there will be little they will not do for you."

"I did not intend to raise myself in their estimation," muttered Elizabeth. "I only wished to ensure Jenny's safety."

"And that is what I love best about you," said William. "There are so many times you take thought for everyone other than yourself. You are one of the most selfless people I have ever met."

Raising herself on her elbow again, Elizabeth gazed at her husband with unfeigned astonishment. "Is that how you see me?"

"How can you think otherwise?" asked William.

"I have as much capacity for selfishness as anyone else."

"Perhaps you do, for none of us are perfect. But when significant events require a choice untainted by self-interest, you can always be counted upon to act in a manner that will benefit others rather than yourself."

When Elizabeth made to protest again, William said: "Take the day's events, Elizabeth. Though you may not have considered the consequences in such a way, there was a real possibility of tragedy today, and not only for little Jenny. If you had not found her or became lost yourself, if you or Jenny had not remembered this shack, events may have come to a different and tragic end."

"Of that, I was well aware," said Elizabeth, shivering at the remembrance of the howling wind and swirling snow, the disorientation and the voices she imagined she heard in the wind. "When I departed the Johnson farm, the weather did not seem as bad as I feared. It soon became worse than I imagined."

"Still, you pressed forward nonetheless," said William. "No one could have faulted you if you had decided the wind and weather were too much and turned back. Yet you continued to press forward, knowing what the consequences could be. 'Greater love hath no man than this, that a man lay down his life for his friends.' Today, you exemplified that verse, Elizabeth. And I could not be prouder that you are my wife."

Feeling embarrassed, Elizabeth burrowed her face into her husband's broad chest. "I do not think I behaved in a manner so heroic as you say. There was nothing else to be done."

"That is why I am convinced I made the right choice in a wife, though we both know I almost botched our chance to be together beyond repair. In the future, however, when these heroic tendencies come over you, I hope you will at least consider me for a moment. My heart almost stopped in my chest when I learned you were out looking for a lost child in this weather."

"I promise I shall do so," said Elizabeth, though she ruined her solemnity when she was forced to stifle a giggle, "if you will promise to take care for your own safety and avoid walking the length of Pemberley in search of your headstrong wife."

"That I cannot do, dear heart. I would go that far and more if it meant I would keep you in my life."

"Then it seems we are alike, William, for I cannot imagine you missing from my life either."

Silence settled about them thereafter, though the crackling of the logs in the hearth kept them company. Soon afterward, William rose to add more fuel to the fire, returning to his previous position when he had completed that task. Soon, the exertions of the day began to make Elizabeth lethargic, and she drifted in and out of consciousness for some time.

"Perhaps," managed she a little later, speaking despite her fatigue, "we should bring our future sons to this place. We should ensure they can start a fire as my father taught me."

"Yes, we shall surely attend to the education of our children. If we should have a girl, I suspect you will insist she is likewise taught this useful skill, for who knows what a mischief a daughter of Mrs. Elizabeth Darcy might get herself into."

"That would be wise, indeed, Husband," said Elizabeth.

As she slipped into slumber, Elizabeth was once again struck by the good fortune of her situation. There was nowhere else in the world she wished to be at that moment than in the arms of her husband in such plain circumstances as they were.

The End

THE KISSING BOUGH MANDATE

Lelia Eye

While doing research, I noted that people in Regency times did not seem to make as big of a deal out of Christmas as we do. I thus decided to come up with a character who would. Initially, I intended to create a random man in the neighborhood to fill the position. Then it occurred to me that there might be an even better choice to fill this role.

To call William Bingley "eccentric" would not have been viewed as a disservice or even an exaggeration by the man himself. Rather, he reveled in his own unpredictable nature and viewed any acknowledgment of his peculiarities as a delight.

But while he could not always remember the proper hierarchy when entering a dining hall and often took his favorite greyhound with him to parties, his perpetual ebullience smoothed over any potential social disasters. Indeed, none of the families with whom he dined in Hertfordshire would ever have said an ill word about him, though they might have spoken of him with exasperation from time to time.

His daughters, Louisa and Caroline, had come to accept his eccentric behavior some time ago, though they absolutely forbade him from showing his face in London. His son, Charles, whose personality and temperament were much milder than his own, did not understand the reason for his sisters' restriction of their father, yet Charles much preferred to remain home at Netherfield regardless, as it kept him close to Jane Bennet. He had fallen madly in love with the young woman a few years before when his father had purchased the estate, yet he had only recently decided to act upon his feelings.

The elder Mr. Bingley had reacted with undeniable joy at the notion, but Charles' sisters had urged him to be cautious. They reminded him of his own impulsivity and encouraged him to elicit the more refined opinion of Mr. Darcy. Mr. Bingley had told his son that if he so wished, they could invite Mr. Darcy and his sister to spend Christmastide with them. And so Charles had written to issue the invitation, Darcy had agreed to come after attending to some business, and the matter was considered settled.

When Mr. Darcy and Georgiana first stepped foot into Netherfield on Christmas Eve, they were both stunned, to say the least.

Doorways, walls, mantles, tables, and various sundry fixtures of the estate house were decorated in evergreen boughs, wreaths covered in red and gold ribbons, sprigs of holly with plump red berries, garlands of effervescent ivy, and various decorative accents fashioned out of paper and silk. Every room bore the scent of cedar and pine, causing Georgiana, though not prone to outbursts, to murmur in surprise to her brother: "It feels as if I have stepped into a forest!"

The elder Mr. Bingley seemed more pleased to see the two Darcys than even his son and daughters were, for he always delighted in showing his Christmas décor to a new audience. Minutes after Darcy and his sister arrived, William Bingley ushered them into the ballroom, where a place of prominence held the item with which he was most delighted.

"This, my dear children," said he, speaking to the Darcys and not to his actual offspring, who had come in behind the pair, "is my kissing bough." His eyes glinted merrily as he tugged at his silver beard, which, though unfashionable, suited him quite well.

"Indeed," said Mr. Darcy uncomfortably, for he was not unfamiliar with such an ornament.

This particular kissing bough had been fashioned from the top of a pine tree and threaded with red, gold, and white ribbons as well as a garland of ivy. The bough had been hung upside-down, and a sprig of mistletoe and holly had been affixed to its center.

"You must be cautious around this most beautiful decoration, Georgiana," said the elder Mr. Bingley, "for I suspect your brother would be quite put out if a young fellow were to give you a kiss."

"There shall be none of that," said Darcy, perhaps a bit too harshly.

Fortunately, his host was not offended. "I have given my son quite the opposite advice, for I have hope that he may have his chance to steal a kiss from Miss Bennet at my Christmas party."

Darcy rather thought such a custom, though common enough, to be inappropriate, even if Mr. Bingley intended the party to be a small one, but he held his tongue. Despite his feelings of aggravation, however, he did not miss the red tinge of embarrassment on Charles Bingley's face at the notion of kissing Miss Bennet in front of others.

Miss Caroline Bingley must have realized how Darcy felt about the matter, as she hastily said: "Papa, I do not believe there is any further need for talk of kissing boughs. I suspect Mr. Darcy has no more than a handful of decorations at Pemberley, for there are very few in England who are as excited about the holiday as you are. No doubt we have given him and his sister quite the shock. I believe they deserve some time to rest before dinner."

"Yes, Papa," said Louisa Hurst, "you must give them some time to themselves. After all, you know Mr. Hurst shall want to try his hand at the card tables later this evening, and our guests shall need their rest if they are not to immediately fall into their beds after eating."

Mr. Bingley grumbled a little but nonetheless agreed, and there was no more talk of the kissing bough that day. But it would not be long before Mr. Darcy would become much more familiar with this particular kissing bough, and his feelings toward it would change quite drastically.

On the morning of Mr. Bingley's Christmas party, which was held four days after the Darcys' arrival at Netherfield, Elizabeth found herself accompanying her mother and Jane on a morning call to Netherfield. Mrs. Bennet had already confirmed through various sources Mr. Darcy's annual income and found herself eager to introduce her daughters to him. Unfortunately for her, she had forced so many calls to Netherfield since the Bingleys' purchase of it that Jane was the only daughter who continued to feel any excitement during the occasion. Elizabeth typically only attended so that she might curb her mother's excesses in front of Charles Bingley.

The three Bennet women found the Bingleys, Hursts, and Darcys already seated within the drawing-room upon their arrival. They were welcomed inside, and once the introductions had been made, Mrs. Bennet saw to it that Jane and Mr. Charles Bingley were speaking together comfortably.

"So, Lizzy," said the elder Mr. Bingley merrily, "what say you of my decorations this year?"

"I believe you have outdone yourself," said Elizabeth with a smile.

"I thought so," said he, pleased, "though I believe I may have given Miss Darcy quite a fright."

Elizabeth turned to Miss Darcy, who seemed uncomfortable to be the focus of attention. "Is that so, Miss Darcy? Well, I can assure you there is no reason to be afraid of what Mr. Bingley says or does. He is the softest-hearted man you shall ever meet. Why, when the puppies of his favorite dog were born, I found Mr. Bingley sitting beside them with a stream of tears running down his face!"

"How unkind, Lizzy!" cried Mr. Bingley. "You know I worried about the pain that Holly must have gone through. She has always been quite sensitive, you know, and eleven children is a most serious matter for any mother to bear."

"Holly was intended to be a hunting dog," said Elizabeth conspiratorially to Miss Darcy, "but Mr. Bingley could not bear to see her facing such a life."

"It is difficult work, you know," said Mr. Bingley, trying but failing to be serious. His mood could hardly ever be truly dampened, but that was most particularly the case around Christmastide.

Miss Darcy gave a small smile which Elizabeth met with one much larger. Though the girl was reserved, it was more than apparent her reticence could be attributed to shyness.

At that moment, Elizabeth decided she wished to befriend Miss Darcy or at least make her more comfortable in Hertfordshire. Jane had advised Elizabeth previously that Miss Darcy usually spent time in company with her companion, but no such woman was in sight. Miss Darcy's companion must have been given leave to spend time with family, which meant Miss Darcy had to have been feeling lonely and out of sorts.

"Do you have other dogs that you use when hunting, then?" asked Mr. Darcy suddenly, looking at the elder Bingley.

Elizabeth provided an answer for Mr. Bingley. "He does not. Gamekeepers despair of his attitude toward dogs--and any living creatures, really."

"Best to leave the hunting for my son," said Mr. Bingley. "Charles is more capable than I am anyway when it comes to that sort of thing."

After that brief exchange, Elizabeth continued to draw Miss Darcy into conversation. The girl was a willing participant, but her reticence was an obstacle that had to be overcome. Nevertheless, Elizabeth remained determined to draw Miss Darcy out.

As Elizabeth continued with her mission, she noticed that Mr. Darcy seemed to be dividing his time between staring at her and staring at Jane. Though she wondered how he might find her and her sister to be so interesting when such a unique character study presented itself in the person of William Bingley, she kept her thoughts to herself.

Once the Bennets left, Darcy had some time before he would need to dress for the Christmas party. He expressed interest in a ride that went unshared by Charles Bingley, so he went riding alone. He needed an opportunity to think, so the solitude was welcome.

The primary purpose for his trip to Netherfield had been to evaluate Jane Bennet as a potential wife for Charles Bingley. Thus far, he had not seen anything to criticize about her character, though he could not be certain she was overly fond of his friend either.

Strangely enough, however, he had found it difficult to concentrate on his evaluation of *Jane* Bennet, as his attention was caught all too often by *Elizabeth* Bennet.

His interest had begun as gratitude. Georgiana, like Darcy himself, was uncomfortable in unfamiliar company, and she tended to withdraw into herself when placed in new situations. With some effort, however, Elizabeth Bennet had managed to encourage Georgiana first to smile and then to offer some unprompted comments here and there. Miss Elizabeth might not have realized it, but such progress for his dear sister was almost miraculous.

Even in the short time he had been in company with Miss Elizabeth, however, his interest had begun to move past appreciation. Her teasing nature was the sort that lightened moods without causing offense, and she lacked the mercenary bent displayed unabashedly by Miss Bingley and many others of society.

Her very presence was refreshing, and Darcy found it difficult to clear her from his mind.

Eventually, Darcy decided to return to Netherfield. It was not long after he turned his horse back that he saw a female figure struggling to carry something in the direction of the manor house.

Frowning, he urged his horse toward the figure at a gallop. As he grew closer, he realized it was Elizabeth Bennet carrying a whimpering greyhound.

When Darcy dismounted nearby, Miss Elizabeth gently placed the dog on the ground. The greyhound let out a light yelp and commenced whimpering once more.

"What happened?" asked Darcy, looking down at the animal.

"Holly hurt her leg somehow," said Miss Elizabeth. "I had decided to walk before readying myself for the Christmas party, and I found Holly limping and crying in a nearby copse of trees."

Darcy allowed himself to take a quick look at the creature. The dog wore a green collar with red circles upon it, the colors no doubt inspired by her namesake, and though she appeared somewhat dirty from frolicking outside, there was no evidence of blood or any sort of need for urgent attention.

He turned his gaze back to Miss Elizabeth. "You should have simply left her and found someone to assist you. She will not perish the moment you leave her."

"I feared that if I left her alone, she might harm herself further or be hurt by some other animal."

"She is only a dog, Miss Bennet. You do not need to hurt yourself in attempting to aid her."

"She is not 'only a dog,'" said the woman with a flash of irritation. "She is quite precious to Mr. Bingley, and his heart would break were anything to happen to her. Besides, I may need to rest a few times, but I am more than capable of carrying a dog."

Darcy looked at Elizabeth Bennet, further protests hovering on his lips. Then he noticed the seriousness in her eyes and the stubborn jut to her chin. He supposed there was no point in further arguing with her. Could he truly admonish her for doing something indicative of a great level of care for others?

"I suppose you are right at that," said Darcy, "but perhaps you may venture to accept my assistance nevertheless. Whereas you have been walking, I have merely been riding my horse. I find myself with an excess of energy at this point. I wonder whether you might allow me to carry the dog back to Netherfield while you lead my horse."

Miss Bennet considered his proposal for a moment before agreeing. Darcy suspected her arms had already tired from carrying the dog, but he did not press the issue. Instead, he kneeled beside the injured animal and began to reach for it.

Ears pressed back, the dog began growling. Miss Elizabeth dropped to her knees and encouraged the creature to become calm, offering soothing strokes and murmuring reassurances. After the dog had settled down, Miss Bennet gave a nod toward Darcy to indicate he could try once more to pick up the creature.

Darcy reached out and slowly took the dog into his arms. Holly gave a yelp when he jostled her leg, but she otherwise simply whimpered as he stood.

"Come, Miss Bennet," said Darcy softly. He watched as she took hold of his horse's reins and began to walk forward, and then he stepped up beside her.

That was the second time that he witnessed Miss Elizabeth's being so caring and attentive that day. There would be a third time. And that would be the time he fell in love with her.

Upon Elizabeth and Mr. Darcy's arrival at Netherfield, Mr. Bingley dropped all of his party preparations to tend to Holly. Judging by how the greyhound's whimpers stopped and the wagging of her tail began, the attention was much appreciated.

Charles Bingley then had to take up the mantle of party preparations along with his sisters, and Mr. Darcy assisted in conveying Elizabeth back to Longbourn.

"I am more than capable of walking back home, Mr. Darcy," said

Elizabeth.

But the gentleman would have none of it. "You shall need time to ready yourself for the party this evening, Miss Bennet. Should you not be able to attend, your presence would be sorely missed."

Elizabeth considered resisting further, but the slight crook of a smile worn by Mr. Darcy and the mild expression of concern in his eyes stayed her protests. "Very well, Mr. Darcy. I shall accept the carriage."

Mr. Darcy's smile widened, and Elizabeth was struck by how handsome the expression was on his face. "I am glad to hear it, Miss Bennet."

"Mr. Darcy," said Elizabeth suddenly, reaching out to touch his arm. They both froze at her action for a few moments, neither certain what to do. Then Elizabeth continued as she had intended and gave his arm a light squeeze. "Thank you for your assistance with Holly."

As Elizabeth began to withdraw her arm, Mr. Darcy caught her hand. She gasped in surprise at the movement, but he did not flinch. Instead, he bowed over her hand and then gently pressed a kiss to her gloved knuckles.

"It was my pleasure, Miss Bennet," murmured he.

As they parted, Elizabeth wondered what was causing her heart to beat so fast. "It must be the excitement of the day," said she to herself, "or perhaps the nigh-overwhelming smell of fresh greenery wafting through the halls of Netherfield."

To Darcy's great relief, only a few families had been invited to Mr. Bingley's Christmas party, which made for a more intimate setting. Of course, when one of the families was as large as that of Mr. Bennet, who had five daughters and a wife whose noise level matched that of at least three guests combined, the room often did seem crowded. Nevertheless, Darcy had been to many a gathering in London with greater numbers and felt this party was at least bearable.

He had agonized over the idea of whether to allow Georgiana to participate in the festivities, but as she had developed a tentative interest in doing so, he had relented. Should there be dancing, however, he had emphasized that she would only be allowed to stand up with the two Bingley men. This plan was quite acceptable to Georgiana, who advised she had no desire to dance at all.

Once all of the guests had arrived, Mr. Bingley insisted that before dinner was to be enjoyed, they must all partake in some games in the ballroom. Charades and Snapdragon passed with no particular issues, but then Mr. Bingley insisted on a game of Hoodman's Blind.

Miss Bingley and Mrs. Hurst attempted to insist that the game was not suitable for the present company, but Mr. Bingley would not be gainsaid, and he was supported in his endeavors by his son and an adamant Mrs. Bennet. "Young people live for games like these," insisted the latter, and William and Charles Bingley agreed wholeheartedly.

An area was created close to the kissing bough for people such as Georgiana and Mr. Bennet to sit, allowing them to observe the game without taking part. Mr. Darcy had also intended to sit out the game with them, but Georgiana had uncharacteristically insisted that he take part, and he had been so surprised by her forcefulness that he had agreed.

The participants drew straws, and a young woman Darcy understood to be Charlotte Lucas selected the shortest straw and was thus blindfolded. After ensuring she could not see around the strip of cloth tied around her head, Mr. Bingley gleefully spun her around three times and then released her.

Miss Lucas reached her hands out to feel whether anyone was nearby, and the laughter, clapping, and taunting of the other guests began.

"Char-lotte," said Miss Elizabeth in a singsong voice, "you are close, but not close enough!"

Miss Lucas lunged forward in an attempt to touch Miss Elizabeth, but the other young woman simply laughed and stepped out of the way. A nearby clap then distracted Miss Lucas, who hastened forward once more in an attempt to touch someone.

Miss Lucas eventually succeeded, and she felt a young woman's face and hair before guessing wrongly at the person's identity.

"You must try again, Charlotte!" cried Miss Elizabeth. Her eyes danced with playful mischief, and her cheeks were flushed due to the effort of staying close to Charlotte while evading her questing hands. She brushed a stray dark-brown curl out of her eyes, the smile on her face filled with such genuine delight that Darcy could scarcely keep himself from staring at her.

Miss Lucas did eventually catch someone and correctly ascertain their identity, and the game continued. This time, a gentleman was blindfolded, and he made such abrupt movements that the other participants' efforts to avoid him bordered on frantic. Such was why

Darcy hastened to move out of the way and did not realize where his steps had taken him.

"Lydia, look!" cried a young woman Darcy believed to be Kitty Bennet. "Mr. Darcy is standing beneath the kissing bough!"

Georgiana gasped audibly, and Darcy, though not typically prone to extreme emotional changes, could have sworn he felt his heart drop to his stomach.

"Ah, yes, certainly, he is," said Sir William Lucas, who had declined to participate in the game. "However, it does not signify. Only unmarried women are to be kissed when they are found beneath a kissing bough. That is the tradition, you know—as is picking a mistletoe berry once a kiss is claimed. We must follow the traditions."

"Oh, what is the fun in all of that, Willy?" asked the elder Mr. Bingley, shaking his head. "I believe a man to be just as susceptible to bad luck if the rules of the kissing bough are disobeyed. Besides, I have always heard that any unmarried lady *or gentleman* who is found beneath it must be kissed. Furthermore, that berry tradition of which you speak is not terribly practical, for the bough is set up so very high, and besides, I believe it to look much more handsome with all its berries intact."

Sir William appeared stunned at having been corrected, but he soon rallied. "I suppose you have the right of it, Billy. We might as well err on the side of caution. There can be no harm in Mr. Darcy's receipt of a kiss from some worthy young woman."

The instant this consensus was reached, Darcy saw Caroline Bingley charging forward to claim the spot of "worthy young woman."

Elizabeth had been near Mr. Darcy and seen him backing toward the spot directly beneath the kissing bough. She had opened her mouth to warn him, but her youngest sister, whose ability to spot opportunities for mischief rivaled a hungry hawk's ability to spy a mouse in a meadow, had called out before she could do anything. When the brief argument over kissing bough traditions resolved, she could sense a certain restlessness in the crowd. Who would be the woman to step forward and claim a kiss from Mr. Darcy?

While she did not know the gentleman very well and suspected he often hid his emotions, there was no mistaking the sudden dread that came over his face as he looked at something behind her. Elizabeth turned and saw Caroline Bingley practically shoving her way through the throng of participants in Hoodman's Blind to reach the gentleman.

More than aware of Caroline's nature—and suspecting, as Mr. Darcy no doubt did, that the young woman would attempt to turn this tradition into something more than it was—Elizabeth made a spur-of-the-moment decision that she would chuckle at in later years.

She stepped forward and joined Mr. Darcy beneath the kissing bough, reaching him mere moments before Caroline did. "I suppose if some young woman must claim a kiss from you, Mr. Darcy, it might as well be someone with whom you are familiar."

Though saying they were familiar with each other was a slight exaggeration, Elizabeth's words produced a nearly instantaneous look of relief on Mr. Darcy's face. The tension seemed to melt from him further as he smiled at her. "I suppose you are correct, Miss Elizabeth."

As he took a step forward, all were quiet, save Caroline, who made an unintelligible noise of protest.

Elizabeth's breath caught in her throat, and she could feel the entire room staring at them. The gentleman brought his hands up and placed them on her cheeks, and then he bowed his head down to kiss the top of her head, his lips gently falling on her hair rather than her bare skin.

Elizabeth, despite herself, had hoped for something more, yet as he withdrew from her, she admired the fact that he respected her enough to keep the kiss as chaste as he could.

She smiled at him, her heart flooding with warmth.

Darcy felt an almost tangible ache as he stepped back from Elizabeth Bennet. He knew of the embarrassment that most young women would feel when being kissed by a gentleman in a room filled with family and friends, yet she had obviously sacrificed herself to save him from Miss Bingley's machinations. He had seen her glance at the other young woman and notice the determination written there. Yet again, Miss Elizabeth had proven herself to be both caring and attentive.

He met her bright smile with one of his own, his heart soaring. But before he could say something to the young woman, he found his attention drawn by a most vociferous protest.

"Wait, wait, wait," cried out Mr. Bingley. "You are doing it all wrong!"

The smile slipped from Miss Elizabeth's face. "I beg pardon?"

"Since Darcy was caught under the kissing bough, *you* are the one who is supposed to do the kissing, Lizzy."

"I—I am?" stuttered the young woman.

"Yes," said Mr. Bingley. "It is the rule, after all."

"Papa," said Miss Bingley urgently, her face scowling most horrendously, "you are most assuredly incorrect. Your understanding of the kissing bough traditions is quite flawed—"

"Is this not my house?" asked Mr. Bingley. "Is this not my kissing bough? Both belong to me, and I hereby mandate that this is how it is to be."

"Papa, you should reconsider—"

"I am decided," declared Mr. Bingley, crossing his arms. "Lizzy, please proceed, if you will."

Miss Elizabeth looked at the man for a moment before she shook her head with an exasperated smile. She turned her attention back to Darcy. "I suppose I must obey our host, Mr. Darcy."

Darcy felt as if his breath had been caught in his throat, and his voice was hoarse as he replied: "I suppose you must."

He stepped toward her, and she reached one hand up to push his neck down even as she stepped up on the tips of her toes to make up for their difference in height. Her face came up next to his head, and he felt a warm puff of air before her soft lips contacted his cheek. Though the kiss was gentle and unassuming, Darcy felt a certainty in his bones that life as he had known it before was over.

He had fallen in love. Irrevocably, wholly, and deeply in love.

He hoped Georgiana would forgive him, but he intended to extend their stay at Netherfield and win Miss Elizabeth's heart. In the depths of his soul, he believed it was the mandate that the kissing bough had given him.

The End

**Thank you for Reading
Mistletoe and Mischief!**

From all of us to all of you, have a very

Merry Christmas!

MORE GREAT TITLES FROM ONE GOOD SONNET PUBLISHING!

PRIDE AND PREJUDICE VARIATIONS

By Jann Rowland

Acting on Faith
A Life from the Ashes (Sequel to Acting on Faith)
Open Your Eyes
Implacable Resentment
An Unlikely Friendship
Bound by Love
Cassandra
Obsession
Shadows Over Longbourn
The Mistress of Longbourn
My Brother's Keeper

By Lelia Eye

Netherfield's Secret

Coincidence
The Angel of Longbourn
Chaos Comes to Kent
In the Wilds of Derbyshire
The Companion
Out of Obscurity
What Comes Between Cousins
A Tale of Two Courtships
Murder at Netherfield
Whispers of the Heart
A Gift for Elizabeth
Mr. Bennet Takes Charge
The Impulse of the Moment
The Challenge of Entail
A Matchmaking Mother
Another Proposal
With Love's Light Wings

PRIDE AND PREJUDICE SERIES

By Jann Rowland

COURAGE ALWAYS RISES: THE BENNET SAGA
The Heir's Disgrace
*Volume II Untitled**
*Volume III Untitled**

By Jann Rowland & Lelia Eye

WAITING FOR AN ECHO
Waiting for an Echo Volume One: Words in the Darkness
Waiting for an Echo Volume Two: Echoes at Dawn

<h1 style="text-align:center">About the Authors</h1>

Jann Rowland

Jann Rowland is a Canadian, born and bred. Other than a two-year span in which he lived in Japan, he has been a resident of the Great White North his entire life, though he professes to still hate the winters.

Though Jann did not start writing until his mid-twenties, writing has grown from a hobby to an all-consuming passion. His interests as a child were almost exclusively centered on the exotic fantasy worlds of Tolkien and Eddings, among a host of others. As an adult, his interests have grown to include historical fiction and romance, with a particular focus on the works of Jane Austen.

When Jann is not writing, he enjoys rooting for his favorite sports teams. He is also a master musician (in his own mind) who enjoys playing piano and singing as well as moonlighting as the choir director in his church's congregation.

Jann lives in Alberta with his wife of more than twenty years, two grown sons, and one young daughter. He is convinced that whatever hair he has left will be entirely gone by the time his little girl hits her teenage years. Sadly, though he has told his daughter repeatedly that she is not allowed to grow up, she continues to ignore him.

Lelia Eye

Lelia Eye has lived in Arkansas all her life. While she enjoys reading and watching movies, she refuses to subject herself to any books or movies with unhappy endings. She has a quirky sense of humor and an irrepressible tendency to play devil's advocate.

Lelia has been interested in writing since she won a short story contest in the sixth grade. Her imagination has been active far longer than that, as her childhood was filled with stories built around such villains as dog-catchers with unflappable determination and pirate ponies with hearts of gold.

Her interest in Jane Austen was sparked when she took a Jane Austen class in college. Her interests span far beyond Jane Austen, however, and encompass the realms of fairy tale, fantasy, and the supernatural.

She lives with her husband of more than ten years and two precious daughters as well as some geriatric fur-babies.

Colin Rowland

Colin Rowland is a Canadian who dislikes cold weather with a passion. This dislike led him to sell his house and move with his wife to the big island of Hawaii, where he loved every minute of the eighteen months they were there. After returning to Canada, he went to work at an international home improvement chain as a contractor consultant.

He currently lives in Calgary with his wife of forty-plus years. Together, they are the proud parents of two sons and two daughters. They also act as servants to two dogs, a Border Collie and a Shih Tzu.

Colin has always loved to read and enjoys almost every genre there is, although his favorites delve into historical periods, from Ancient Rome to World War Two and everything in between. His interest in the works of Jane Austen began with advice from his brother, author Jann Rowland, to read *Pride and Prejudice*. Inspired by Austen's work, Colin now spends his free time penning manuscripts centered around the Regency England period.

Please Jann, Lelia, and Colin them know what you think or sign up for their mailing list to learn about future publications:

Website:	http://onegoodsonnet.com/
Facebook:	https://facebook.com/OneGoodSonnetPublishing/
Twitter:	**@OneGoodSonnet**
Mailing List:	http://eepurl.com/bol2p9

Made in the USA
Monee, IL
07 July 2026